THE DEAL

Tony Malcolm was broke, down-at-the-heels and desperate. What he wanted more than anything else in the world was a drink.

The local bar owner set him a price.

"Shoot yourself," he said, and handed Malcolm a revolver.

Malcolm drank, put the gun to his head and pulled the trigger. When the gun misfired, the bar owner pressed his claim. Since Malcolm had failed to kill himself, he still owed the bar owner a death, and the bar owner had just the victim in mind.

A CHOICE OF ASSASSINS

A brilliant novel of shame and murder.

Books by William McGivern

ODDS AGAINST TOMORROW
MENTION MY NAME IN MOMBASA
(with Maureen McGivern)
SAVAGE STREETS
SEVEN LIES SOUTH
KILLER ON THE TURNPIKE
ROAD TO THE SNAIL
POLICE SPECIAL
A PRIDE OF PLACE

Published by Bantam Books

A CHOICE OF ASSASSINS
WILLIAM P. McGIVERN

BANTAM BOOKS · TORONTO · NEW YORK · LONDON

A CHOICE OF ASSASSINS

*A Bantam Book / published by arrangement with
Dodd, Mead & Company, Inc.*

PRINTING HISTORY
*Dodd, Mead edition published October 1963
Serialized by Newspaper Enterprise Association
Bantam edition published October 1964*

*Bantam Books are published by Bantam Books, Inc. Its trade-mark,
consisting of the words "Bantam Books" and the portrayal of a
bantam, is registered in the United States Patent Office and in other
countries. Marca Registrada. Printed in the United States of America. Bantam Books, Inc., 271 Madison Ave., New York 16, N. Y.*

1

HE sat burning on the dark sands of a beach in southern Spain. The sand stretched like a border of dirty lace at the foot of a fishing village called Cartama. In front of him was the flat sea, and the sharp reflection of sunlight from its surface struck painfully at his red-rimmed eyes; behind him were the rolling, elephant-colored mounds of the Sierra Nevada mountains; inside him was a thirst that he knew would soon become dangerous.

There were noise and color a hundred yards off to his right, and the high-pitched talk and laughter of tourists mingled with the cries of waiters serving drinks and shrimps and sardines from the weathered bars at the foot of the gentle slope which led up to the village.

Young girls in bikinis were stretched out like oiled bronze statues under the clear sun; children swooped about like excited birds among the gaudy umbrellas and beach huts; a group of young men were swimming out to sea, their brown arms flashing through the blue water with a lazy, confident rhythm. Far beyond the swimmers the white sails of fishing boats skimmed gracefully against the blue sky.

The man folded his arms over his knees and put his head down on his crossed wrists. The sun formed a layer of shimmering heat on his dirty white suit. Flies buzzed about his ears. He was isolated from the pleasant, noisy activity of the beach; no one came near him, no one seemed curious about him; he sat alone in the heat.

Suddenly he became aware of a strange object at his feet. It was round and red, shining with drops of water.

A voice said tentatively, "That's my ball."

He raised his head slowly, and felt the glare of the sun on

his eyes and face. The light hurt his eyes. He blinked and wet his cracked lips.

A child stood six feet from him, a thin, blonde girl who wore yellow shorts and an unnecessary sash about her flat brown chest. She watched him with grave blue eyes, a faint frown on her small face. In one hand she held a half-full bottle of orange-flavored soda water.

"All right," he said. "It's your ball."

She took a step forward toward him, as cautious as a wild creature. Then she stopped.

"Could you throw it to me, please?"

"All right." He rolled the red ball across the sand, and she stooped and picked it up, her movements surprisingly quick and graceful.

"Thank you," she said. "I have to go now."

She turned away, then hesitated and glanced back at him, an uncertain frown shadowing her grave eyes; it was as if she realized there might have been a haste, an incompleteness, in their exchange.

"Thank you very much," she said. "I threw it toward the water. But I can't throw very straight. It rolled over here."

"All right, okay," he said, without moving his painfully cracked lips.

"Why are you always so dirty?" she asked him politely, and rested one foot on top of the other to gain a moment's relief from the burning sand.

Not so long ago, he thought—months, maybe even weeks —this sort of thing could have brought tears to his eyes. But no more. All irrelevant emotion had been scoured out of him, brutally and finally; he was as clean and empty as if the job had been done with sandpaper and blow torches. But soon he would need a drink to anesthetize the one area the sandpaper and blow torches couldn't reach, and it was then he noticed the bottle of soda the child was holding in a thin brown hand. He connected it shrewdly to the bars at the foot of the slope which led to the village.

"What's your name?"

"Jennifer. Jennifer Davis. What's yours?"

"Tony. Tony Malcolm. Do people call you Jenny?"

She sighed. "Yes."

"Jenny's a pretty name. Tony and Jenny. How about that? Our names rhyme. You're American, too, I'll bet."

"Yes. We're staying here a month. My mother doesn't

like Spain, she says. She got sick from the food the first week we were here, and the doctor didn't speak any English."

Tony Malcolm smiled up at her and he pushed a black strand of sand-stiffened hair from his forehead. He was thirty-two years old; his lips were cracked, his cheeks unshaven, his eyes bleary and red-rimmed; but the smile, which was bold and practiced, caught the little girl's interest.

"Let me tell you a secret, Jenny," Tony Malcolm said, leaning forward slightly—not enough to frighten her or cause her to draw away from him, but just enough to emphasize the artful threads of humor and excitement which were woven together in the soft, conspiratorial tones of his voice. "I'll tell you why I'm always dirty. When I was a little boy, about your age, I had a very strict governess. She was always marching me up to the bathroom to scrub my ears, and pulling me inside to change my clothes. She was a terrible woman. Ugly as a witch." Malcolm lowered his voice theatrically, and the little girl's eyes widened in helpless fascination.

"Was she really ugly?" she said, in a soft, breathless voice.

"She'd make any witch you ever saw look like a movie star. But the worst part of it was the scrubbing and washing, morning, noon, and night." Malcolm shrugged humorously. "When I grew up, I decided to stop all that nonsense. No more changing my clothes three times a day." He smiled at her, confidently and cheerfully. "I'm dirty because I like to be dirty, Jenny. Now you know my secret. Aren't there things you'd like to do? But can't? Because there's always somebody to stop you?"

"I don't know." She glanced uneasily over her shoulder, as if she were afraid of being seen or overheard by the distant groups of tourists sunning themselves among the bright cluster of beach umbrellas. Then, obviously reaching a decision, she squatted on her heels in front of him, and said in a serious, matter-of-fact voice: "Well, it doesn't make any difference. Because you can't do what you want when you're young. You have to wait till you're old, like you."

Malcolm scooped up a handful of sand and let it trickle idly through his fingers. "Poor Jenny," he said, with humorous solicitude. Then, very casually, he let his eyes turn to the bottle she was holding. "Where did you get that?"

"From back there," she said, swinging around to indicate the tourist area of the beach. "From the bar, from Manuel."

"Did you pay him for it?"

3

"No, I've got credit," she said seriously. "For two bottles a day, one in the morning and one in the afternoon."

"You just go up to the bar and ask for a bottle of soda and Manuel gives it to you?"

She nodded importantly, obviously pleased by his mildly incredulous expression. "One in the morning, one in the afternoon."

"Would Manuel give you anything else if you asked for it?"

"Like what?"

"Oh, a sandwich, shrimps, sardines. Would he?"

"Well, we eat at the hotel. We're on *pensione*." She pronounced the word to rhyme with "mention."

"But supposing you asked him?"

"I guess he would. I don't know."

Malcolm felt a cold knot of anxiety tightening in his stomach. "Supposing you asked him for a bottle of wine, Jenny? What do you think he'd say?"

"I couldn't do that," she said, widening her eyes with a suggestion of virtuous surprise. "My mother won't even let me have a sip of wine or beer. Some of the kids here do, but Mommy says it's just showing off, starting something there's plenty of time for later."

Goddamn her, Malcolm thought, wearily and sullenly; a feeble, frustrating anger was burning inside him now.

"I didn't say anything about you drinking the wine," he said, and his smile was so wide that it hurt his sunburned lips and cheeks. "I just thought we'd play a little joke on your mommy."

"You know her?" She tilted her head to one side, watching him skeptically.

"Sure." Malcolm risked everything on a guess. "Your mother's divorced, isn't she?"

Jenny studied him with frank interest. "Yes, Daddy had his head turned," she said, with a small, practiced sigh. "He misses us terribly, but he had to leave us. It's like being sick, Mommy says. He can't help himself. He should have been locked up, she says."

Malcolm held his breath for an instant, trying desperately to think of another prop to buttress her slowly growing confidence in him. He was dizzied by the good luck of his first guess; his heart boomed like surf in his ears, but that didn't matter, nothing mattered now, for he could almost feel the smooth cool curve of a wine bottle cradled in his hands. But he was still trembling at the chance he had taken; the village was full of divorced women, and most of them

4

seemed to be accompanied by small female children named Debby or Linda or Jenny—but still, he might have been wrong. . .

"That's why your mommy's sad at times," he said, softly and caressingly, trying to cast his voice like a gentle net over the wings of her emotions and will. "It makes her feel sad to think of your daddy. It makes her cry, doesn't it?"

Jenny stared thoughtfully at the bright sea. "No, but she swears about him a lot, when we're in docks or stations, and the luggage gets lost or something. Or when he doesn't send us what he's supposed to in the mail."

She turned her narrow blonde head from the sea and studied Malcolm thoughtfully. She was a far from stupid child; during her small span of years she had heard sufficient baffling argument and recrimination between her parents to convince her that trying to understand the adult world was a waste of time. Therefore she had focused her curiosity and speculation on the smaller and more manageable area of her own feelings and reactions. And now she wondered why Malcolm interested her. It wasn't the way she felt about small kittens and birds with broken wings. She knew and vaguely understood that reaction, and she didn't like it. It made her feel helpless, and she didn't like that at all. But this was different. She knew Malcolm wanted something from her, hungrily and desperately, but she couldn't figure out what it was. He looked hot and smudged, sitting there on the sand. *Smudged,* that was just the word. His dark, sulky face, with the cracked lips and red-rimmed eyes, looked as if a broad thumb had been pressed against it, so that his frowns and smiles were all blurred and unnatural. There was sweat on his forehead, little blisters of it under the strands of coarse black hair, and when they trickled down into his eyebrows they gleamed there like tiny jewels in the sunlight. And his eyes were bright and tense as they searched her face. A man had looked at her like that in the park one day. and her mother had dragged her off, tight-lipped and furious, but this was different somehow, different from the well-dressed old man in the park who had asked so politely and nervously if he could adjust the bandage on her knee.

"I was thinking we might play a little joke on your mother," Malcolm said. "To make her laugh, to cheer her up."

She knew he was lying then, but she said, "What kind of a joke?"

"Well, I'll tell you," he said, smiling and rubbing a hand

5

across his face. The sun was a mile-high lance probing his skull. He couldn't think of anything to say; words skittered about like mice inside his blazing head. "I bought her a drink one night, that's the joke," he said, laughing weakly. "There were lots of us sitting around the Quita Pena, and I bought her a drink, and I said to her, to your mommy, I said, 'Now you wait and see, one of these days you're going to buy me a bottle of wine, and you won't even know it.' " Malcolm stared at the little girl and blinked his eyes quickly, for her blonde body and blonde hair had begun to shimmer and twist before him in the maddening rays of the sun. It was as if a flaming curtain had fallen between them, consuming her small body before his eyes. He felt a wrench of panic. What had he said to her? Something about drinks. He began to laugh, trying to remember what he had said to her. "It's funny, very funny," he said helplessly, and then his voice trailed off, for his mind had become a roaring blank.

"Why is that funny?" Jenny asked him.

"It's a grown-up kind of joke," Malcolm said desperately. "But it would be very funny if you go to Manuel right now, and tell him you want him to give you—*insist* that he give you—" Malcolm pounded a fist weakly on the sand. "—a bottle, a liter of wine for your mother and some of her friends. Then bring it to me. And it will be very funny, you see, when we tell her about it."

"I don't think you know my mother at all," Jenny said, and got deliberately to her feet. "I think you just want me to get a bottle of wine for you. Steal it for you, that's what it amounts to. And I don't think you're dirty because you like to be. You're dirty because you can't help it. You haven't told me the truth at all."

Malcolm tried with extreme care to gauge his need for a drink. He decided after laborious calculations that he was good for another hour at least, and that he might as well spend that time sitting quietly in the sun. He thought of the bars in the village. The Quita Pena, the Seville, the Central. Somewhere he'd find a drink. Meanwhile he was all right. He wouldn't move. He was fine. He wouldn't even crawl into the shade. This was fine. There were no memories yet, no pain at all.

"Well, isn't that true?" Jenny said hesitantly. "I mean, you did lie to me, didn't you? You didn't tell me the truth."

Malcolm raised his head and blinked his eyes, confused by the sound of her voice. He had thought she had gone away. "Truth?" he said in a thick, puzzled voice. "I don't know

6

any." The words were so soft and blurred that Jenny leaned forward with a quick, birdlike gesture in an attempt to understand them. Her complacent indignation was melting away. She blinked her eyes against sudden, stinging tears as she saw the flies buzzing about his dark head, and the drops of perspiration gleaming like precious jewels on his eyelashes. As he stared at her blankly, Jenny knew he didn't recognize her, that he had forgotten all about her. With that awareness the unwelcome warmth penetrated the depths of her being and swelled close to the cold, invulnerable area which she imagined as being the exact center of her body, and which she had always fought to keep safe and inviolate from everybody in the world.

"I'll get it for you," she said, and her voice trembled with pain and compassion. "I'll get the wine. I will, really I will."

Malcolm swallowed with a great effort. "Yes, yes," he said. "A liter, remember. A liter of red. Hurry."

As she wheeled about and ran across the hot sand toward the cluster of beach umbrellas, Malcolm stared after her, hopefully and anxiously. Prayers formed in his mind. Prayers for her safe return. She had started a dangerous journey, and a hundred pitfalls waited to trap her quick, slender body. Everything she encountered was shimmering with an evil, seductive radiance. The glistening hides of tourists spread-eagled under the sun, the flash and snap of bright umbrellas in the breeze, the roar of white breakers and the splintered reflections from the glass-filled trays of waiters—all this noise and light threatened to engulf and destroy her darting little figure.

He pounded a fist helplessly on the hot sand. Words of encouragement broke hoarsely in his mind. Don't talk to anybody; keep away from them; run, run, run. . . . A vivid streak of rage shot through his coiling thoughts as a black-haired youngster blocked her path. He was a head taller than Jenny and his chest and shoulders were the color of chocolate from the sun. The boy's teeth flashed in a smile as he put his hands on Jenny's shoulders and turned her toward the water.

Damn you, Malcolm thought, damn you, let her go! His fist was raw from pounding against the gritty sand. But Jenny slipped away from the boy and ran on toward Manuel's bar, and when Malcolm saw that she was safe he cheered exuberantly, as if a horse with his life's savings on it had roared home a winner. You're a sweetheart, he thought, almost weeping with gratitude. Nothing could stop her now, he knew; she was free as an arrow shot from a bow.

She was talking to Manuel at the bar, pointing off toward the cluster of beach umbrellas, and when Malcolm saw this evidence of her shrewdness, he hugged himself tightly, compressing all his hope and happiness in the small circle of his own two arms.

It would work, it had to work, he thought; she was so clever, so loyal, nothing on earth could stop her. Already Manuel had turned to the ice-packed crate where he kept his wine. He lifted out a shining liter of the red and gave it to Jenny, who cradled the bottle in her arms, flashed a smile at him, and then wheeled and ran back across the hot sands toward Malcolm.

Malcolm rested his head on his crossed arms and closed his eyes. He was trembling helplessly; the strain had been so great that his body felt slack and useless, as if it had just been released from a rack. He drew careful mouthfuls of air into his lungs, restoring himself and preparing himself for the annealing comfort being borne to him in the child's slender arms.

Jenny's mother said sharply, "Just where do you think you're going with that bottle of wine?"

Jenny stopped so abruptly that she almost lost her balance. Turning her head she saw her mother standing a dozen feet from her, at the end of the wooden foot-walk which led from the village onto the beach.

"Hi," Jenny said, with a bright, guilty smile.

Jenny's mother was named Coralee. She was a tall young woman with natural blonde hair and a thoughtlessly pretty face. She wore a high-crowned straw hat, flaring black sunglasses, and a bikini which was no more than a colorful welt across her brown, sloping hips. She carried a book and a floppy beach bag with circular wooden handles.

"I asked you a question," she said irritably. "What are you doing with that bottle of wine? I've told you a dozen times, if I told you once, that I expect you to behave yourself when I leave you alone on the beach."

Coralee Davis was not in a particularly cheerful mood, and the spectacle of her child running about with a bottle of wine in her scrawny arms added sharply to the burden of her exasperation. She had eaten too much *paella* at lunch, and her siesta had been plagued with thick, sluggish dreams which left her with an irritating headache. Awakening in the rooms she shared with Jenny, she had sponged herself inadequately in the trickle of water from the shower and then, feeling

8

somewhat better, she had gone to Seville where Paco had told her to meet him that afternoon. But Paco hadn't shown up. She had waited an hour before returning to the *pensione* and changing for the beach.

Jenny was saying something. "What's that?" her mother said sharply. "Speak up, for heaven's sake."

"I was taking it to him," Jenny said, nodding over the neck of the wine bottle toward Malcolm, who sat with his head on his crossed arms about fifty yards from them.

Coralee Davis looked suspiciously at the figure in the soiled white suit. Then she looked grimly in the opposite direction, toward the cluster of beach umbrellas and sun-soaked tourists, as if silently calling on them to witness her indignation.

"Did he give you the money to pay for it?"

"No, Mommy. He said he knew you. And that it was a joke for me to get it from Manuel." Jenny regretted having to tell the truth. She had wanted to help Malcolm. But now the price was too high. "I'm sorry," she said, putting a small catch in her voice. "But he said it was just a joke."

"The idea!" Coralee took the bottle from Jenny's arms, gripping it by the neck as if she wanted to strangle it. With her free hand she spun her daughter about and marched her helplessly toward Manuel's weatherbeaten little bar.

Malcolm looked up then. His heart lurched heavily as he saw Jenny moving away from him, her slender body almost hidden by a tall blonde woman who was pushing her resolutely toward the tourists' area of the beach. He raised his hand and tried to call out to them, but he couldn't find the words he wanted in his spinning thoughts. The sounds he made were only inarticulate chokings of rage and despair.

Then he braced his weight on one hand and stared blindly at the immense, glittering sea.

2

BUT by seven o'clock that night, through a stroke of pure luck, Malcolm was safely and comfortably drunk. He had left the beach at six to begin his rounds of the village bars, and had struck gold at his first stop, the Quita Pena. Without being asked, he had joined a table of Americans who were examining a German camera which a bearded young man named Jeff was thinking of buying. Malcolm had earned Jeff's gratitude—and four large brandies—by pointing out that the original lens had been replaced by an inferior make. "The leather case, the filter, and timers aren't important," he had said, making a desperate effort to speak clearly and concisely. "Without the original lens it's just a box, an engagement ring without a diamond."

Malcolm was not too surprised at his own alertness, nor by the bearded young man's gratitude. When he needed a drink badly he could usually trust some instinct or intuition to lead him to it. He sat nibbling the remains of sausage and bread which the Americans had left behind them, quite comfortable now with the brandy drugging his mind and blurring his thoughts. There were a half-dozen Spaniards standing along the small bar. They paid no attention to Malcolm. He sat alone putting bits of food slowly into his mouth. and thinking of how he would get through the rest of the night.

The fishing village of Cartama was on the coastal road that twisted along the Mediterranean from Málaga to Gibraltar. It was halfway between those points, a village of a thousand souls, an ugly church, a half-dozen bars, and rows of shops and *pensiones* huddled together on the narrow streets which stretched like the spokes of a wheel from the central plaza.

It rested flatly on the sloping ledge of rock which slanted down to the beach. No crown of white villas adorned the mountain ranges above Cartama. The tourist flood had not swollen the village into a miniature Biarritz or Cannes; unlike many booming towns up and down the coast, Cartama was still cheap, still poor, and the trickle of foreigners who eddied about its rough beaches and primitive *pensiones* were searching for economy in the sun rather than comfort or glamor.

Malcolm thought about the Bar Seville. He owed them money. Antonio had sent him away the last three or four times he had gone there. But when Antonio went home for supper, his borther-in-law, Miguel, would be in charge. Miguel was stupid and sentimental, and he might give another bottle of wine. The Cantina? They had his cameras and most of his luggage, but even that didn't cover what he owed them.

There was Domingo's place in the hills, but he knew he could never walk that far. And he was afraid of Domingo.

Malcolm sat perfectly still, conserving his strength. He was fine now. There was nothing to worry about. And in time a way to get through the night would occur to him. . . .

It was one o'clock in the morning when Malcolm was ushered gently but firmly from the Bar Seville. He didn't care; he cared about nothing now, for he was thoroughly and invulnerably drunk, and he knew he would be able to sleep for hours on the warm beach. As he had hoped, poor Miguel had given him a bottle of wine, and when Antonio returned from supper, his disgust at his brother-in-law had taken the form of derisive generosity to Malcolm; he had placed a bottle of brandy on the bar and scornfully urged him to drink his fill on the house. For the last time . . . .

Malcolm walked slowly and carefully down the narrow street to the beach. It was dark and quiet now, except for the murmur of waves, the faint stars in the sky, and the occasional bursts of soft laughter from behind shuttered windows.

It was at the drinking fountain of the burros, where the street turned toward the beach, that Malcolm lost his footing and fell sprawling across the gutter.

The fall seemed to take forever; he was clearly conscious of his twisting ankle, and the pleasant weightlessness that came with a loss of balance, and then the leisurely, slow-motion descent of his limp body to the ground. The crash of his forehead against the cobblestones of the street terminated the sequence like a vivid exclamation point.

When Malcolm opened his eyes the cool gray light of dawn was in the street, and he found himself looking into the open mouth of a dead fish. The fish was very small, a mere streak of silver in the filth of the gutter, but Malcolm's face was so close to it that he could see a faint pearly light behind its eyes and the beautifully etched shadings of blue and white along the sides of its body.

Even in the cool air of early morning the fish smelled bad, and he thought it strange that the cats hadn't got to it yet.

"Man, what happened?"

The words were Spanish, the voice was thick and cheerful. Footsteps sounded near him and a hand shook his shoulder. "You hurt, friend?"

Malcolm pushed himself up and sat on the curbstone. The man sat beside him and patted his shoulder clumsily.

He said again, *"Hombre, qué pasa?"*

He was a fisherman, a young man with a flushed face and happy eyes. His cheeks were black with whiskers, and he smelled of wine.

Malcolm took his arm. "I need a drink. Do you have anything to drink?"

The man laughed softly. "It's all inside me. All inside me."

"Your house? Is there any there? Any money?"

"No, only my wife is at my house."

The man started to rise, but Malcolm tightened his grip on his arm. "I must have something to drink," he said. "Please help me." There was an edge of panic in his voice. The blow on his head had somehow diminished the effects of the brandy.

The man shook his head gravely. "The bars are closed, and I have no wine or money." Then he belched sleepily and looked at Malcolm. For a moment it seemed as if he were trying to remember something, for his eyes became distant and vague, and a frown toched his forehead. Then he giggled softly and suggestively, and nudged Malcolm with his elbow. "Go and see the whore, eh?" He winked and made gestures with his hands, his face lighting up with wistful desire. "I have never had the courage," he said sadly. "We talk about it in the boats, all of us talk about it, but no one has enough courage. Or money," he added with a philosophical shrug. The innocent prurience faded from his features, and he sighed deeply and wearily as he looked at his bare feet. "How could I make her smile?"

"Don't talk to me about whores," Malcolm said tensely. "I need a drink."

The man smiled, and his eyes became soft with a dream. "She is good to anyone who will make her smile. I have heard it, and I believe it is true. But how could I make her smile? I have no shoes. Do you realize that, Señor?"

"Goddamit, can't you hear me?" Malcolm shook the man's arm, roughly and violently. "I need something to drink."

The man pulled himself free and lurched to his feet, his face was full of stupid alarm. "You hurt your head, you are bleeding," he said in a worried voice, and then he turned and hurried down the street toward the beach, occasionally glancing back over his shoulder at Malcolm as if to reassure himself that the figure huddled on the curb was real and true, and not just a fancy of his imagination.

Malcolm stood up and looked about tensely and fearfully; it was the way a man in a death cell might react to the sound of booted feet, a slippery metallic rush of chains, the creaking of a heavy iron door. Ahead and behind him the street was empty and quiet, a pearl-gray tunnel leading from the mountains to the sea.

The face of a woman appeared in the mists of his mind. And on her face was a smile. Slowly at first the face began to circle against the blackness inside his head, but soon the movement became so violent and rapid that the features blurred beyond recognition, and there was only a brilliant light spinning against his skull like a buzz saw. Malcolm gasped at the pain. He sank to his knees in front of the burros' drinking fountain and rubbed his forehead savagely against its cast-iron sides. The pain inside him grew monstrously. In his anguish some instinct or intuition dredged up the words of the fisherman, and he seized on them frantically.

He crawled to his feet and splashed the cool water from the fountain over his face, sluicing dirt from his whiskered face and rubbing away the wine at the corners of his mouth.

She lived in the mountains a few miles above Cartama, at a place called the Arroyo de Miel, the river of honey. The name had nothing to do with the geraniums and oleanders blooming there, but with the fact that the small cluster of shops and buildings had once been owned by a man who kept bees. Malcolm knew her name, but he had never seen her in the village. As he turned and started unsteadily up the street toward the Arroyo de Miel, he prayed that what the fisherman had told him was true.

To climb the curving road through the mountains to the Arroyo de Miel was no challenge to the young tourists who visited Cartama. In the cool of the morning or evening it was no more than a pleasant hike. The soft peaks of the mountains stood out clearly against the white sky, sparkling with rose and lemon lights at dawn and streaked with cool purple shadows as the sun dipped behind them at night. When the wind came off the sea it was possible to reach the Arroyo de Miel without working up a sweat.

But to Malcolm, sustained only by a mixture of delirium and hope, the trip was agony. There were flowers along the road, birds wheeling in the fine dry air, and lances of sunlight breaking their tips against the rosy sides of the hills, but Malcolm saw only the bitter rocky road at his feet, or the rough bark of a tree as he rested his cheek against it and waited for his heart to stop pounding like an imprisoned animal against his chest.

He would never have made it except for one miraculous stroke of luck; a refrigerated truck with a load of fresh fish for Madrid lumbered past him in low gear, and before it picked up speed Malcolm lurched forward and got a grip on the ropes that were lashed across the tailgate.

The truck pulled Malcolm nearly half the way to the Arroyo de Miel. The rope cut deeply into the palms of his hands and the rocks on the road were sharp under his broken shoes. But he didn't care. Something was helping him, and he was numbly grateful. The truck seemed big and strong and friendly. Drops of salty water splashed from the tarpaulin onto his face, refreshing and sustaining him, and the powerful throb of the motor was like a support for his own laboring heart. But gradually the truck picked up speed. Malcolm ran to keep up with it. He told himself not to let go. But it was no use. When the driver shifted down into third the truck leaped forward smoothly and eagerly, jerking Malcolm off his feet. He hung on desperately for another twenty or thirty yeards, his shoes scraping noisily over the loose pebbles and rocks but then his hands slipped from the rope, and he stumbled and fell forward on his face. He lay beside the road, breathing in the dust stirred up by the truck, with the sun beating on his back and the taste of blood in his mouth, trying to remember why he was climbing this torturous hill to the Arroyo de Miel.

He continued walking. At the top of a shallow rise he saw what seemed to be a mirage; something long and brilliant flashed against the mountainside, sparkling with lights, roaring with noise. The motor was louder now. It was an American car, a slim, blue convertible, crowded with people. The sun blazed on the sleek chrome decorations, sparkled on headlights and hubcaps. Malcolm heard the people in the car shouting and laughing. He had a dazzling impression of white teeth and slim brown throats corded with excitement and laughter. In the back seat a boy in a white shirt was drinking from a bottle, and a girl lay against him with her bare legs hanging outside the car. The car went by Malcolm as slowly as if it were drifting through a dream, triumphant with light and color. The boy waved at Malcolm and threw his bottle into the air. Time seemed suspended as it drifted lazily toward the ground. Malcolm saw that it was half-full, and he watched the bottle disappear into the clouds of dust swept up by the car with only the sound of breaking glass to tell him where it had struck the road.

The car roared away, and Malcolm knelt beside the spreading brown stain in the dust, rubbing his fingers over it and touching them to his lips. It was brandy, a pint or more of it, being sucked greedily into the hard, dry earth. He knelt beside the brown stain for a long time, staring at it with sullen, bewildered anger.

When he came to the Arroyo de Miel, it was seven o'clock in the morning. The tiny village was a heap of white buildings which looked as if they had been swept up carelessly against the side of the mountain. At the top of the single street was Domingo's bar, a low whitewashed building with beaded curtains hanging at the doors and windows. Domingo's was flat against the mountain, its heavy beams driven deep into the solid rock. There was no church in the village, only a scattering of homes, a few shops that sold milk and coffee and tobacco, and a sagging kiosk for newspapers and lottery tickets.

Yellow dogs lay in the dusty street, and on the tables of a sidewalk cafe the flies crawled about with an air of sluggish confidence. An old man was drinking coffee, and Malcolm said to him, "Please, tell me where Tani lives?"

The old man looked at Malcolm, and his face under a fine moss of whiskers hardened with contempt. "You don't need a woman," he said. "You need to sleep."

"Tell me, please," Malcolm said weakly. The sun was so heavy on his back and the bruise on his forehead was throbbing so painfully that he found it difficult to put his thoughts into words. "Please, where is she?"

The old man's face changed as he studied Malcolm. He pointed with his cane toward an alley. "Go down there. It's not far. It's on the left. It's not hard to find." He rubbed a hand over his mouth and where his lips parted a single gold tooth flashed in the sun. "There are flowers in the window."

Malcolm didn't remember walking away from the old man. Somehow he found her home. He stood on a stone step pounding weakly on a wooden door. There was a fragrance of geraniums in the air, mingling with the smell of olive oil and dust, and he saw blood-red flowers which stood like prisoners on the sill of a barred window.

"Go away," a man's voice said. "She is sleeping."

Malcolm stared helplessly at the man who stood in the open doorway, sleeves rolled up above the elbows of his thick, hairy arms, and a cigarette plastered against his lower lip. He was about forty, stocky and muscular, with small brown eyes embedded deeply in his broad face.

15

"I have to see her, I must," Malcolm said weakly. "I walked up here, all the way from Cartama."

"It will be easier walking back, it's downhill," the man said. He did not look at Malcolm, but stared up and down the street, and at the sea and the clouds, examining the portents of the new day with a clinical frown.

"But I can make her smile," Malcolm said. He was near tears. "That's why I came here. To make her smile."

"Go away," the man said, still scanning the sky and sea with a sailor's eyes. "She is sleeping."

From somewhere behind him a woman's voice said quietly, "Bring him in, Jorge," and Malcolm felt his heart pound with hope because he knew that intuition and instinct had once again performed their customary miracle.

The room was small and clean with windows facing on the sea. There was no rug on the tile floor, only twin studio couches, a deep chair with a large ottoman in front of it, and a low round table on which a collection of tiny plastic animals were arranged in realistic groups. The cattle gazed in a herd on the shiny surface of the coffee table and the sheep were quartered separately, safely beyond the reach of a tidy pack of red and white wolves. Tani wore faded blue jeans, a man's white shirt, and sandals made of thongs and flat pieces of supple leather. She was small and slim, with thick black hair and eyes that were dark and slick as cherries against her smooth brown skin.

"Who told you I like to be amused?" she asked Malcolm in a low voice. She spoke English with a faint accent; she spaced the words with care, but sounded the terminal consonants with an obvious effort.

Malcolm tried to collect his thoughts. "I heard you were grateful to anyone who made you smile," he said.

Tani sat in the deep chair and crossed her ankles on the footstool. She let her hands hang limply over the arms of the chair. She wore no make-up at all, her face was scrubbed clean as a child's, but there were heavy silver bracelets on both of her narrow wrists, and a pendant glittered at the base of her throat; her small, expressionless face was like the stillness at the core of a cyclone, an area of almost unnatural quietness intensified by the flash and glitter of her necklace and bracelets.

"Who told you that?" she asked Malcolm.

"An Englishman, a tall and very proper Englishman." That was clever, that would impress her, he thought; she must have memories of lank young Britishers in white flannels, playing tennis at clubs her family could only enter through the back doors. "He told me you had been kind to him because he had amused you," Malcolm said. "He spoke of you with great respect."

Tani continued to stare impassively at him, but there was something different about her eyes now, a sharpening of interest, and a hint of cruelty or speculation. Finally she said, "You are going to amuse me? Make me smile?"

"Yes, yes, that's it," Malcolm said excitedly. He paced the clean bare floor and rubbed the back of a hand across his mouth. "That's why I came here," he said, trying desperately to make his thoughts march in orderly columns. "I know a fabulous story, a terribly funny story. And it's true. I swear before God it's true."

"Tell it to me," she said.

Malcolm looked at her pleadingly. "And if you think it's funny, will you give me something to drink?"

"You don't want to go to bed with me?"

"No, no," he said, shaking his head desperately. "I only want something to drink."

"Very well, let me hear the story."

"Yes, of course," Malcolm said. He began pacing again, staring helplessly at the walls, at the wide expanse of sea that stretched beyond the windows. What could he tell her? He could think of nothing, his mind was empty, a roaring vacuum. But then, so abruptly that it startled him, the name of a dog he had once known blazed in his thoughts as clearly and vividly as a brand burned into soft white wood. Toto! That was the dog's name, a miniature French poodle, dyed a hideous shade of blue. Malcolm laughed boisterously. "You'll love this," he said to Tani. "It's a story about a dog, a ridiculous little dog named Toto." But what happened to the dog, he wondered helplessly. What was funny about Toto? He must be dead now, for all this happened a long time ago. But there was something funny about the little dog. There must be.

"Well," Tani said skeptically. "What about the little dog?"

"I'm just trying to remember the details." Malcolm said. All of his strength seemed to be flowing away; his hands were trembling and his knees felt as if they were about to collapse under him. "I'm trying to decide the best way to tell you about Toto. I don't want to cheat you." Then, even as he was speaking, another name flashed in his mind: Bill Harvey. The funny thing about Toto had happened to Bill Harvey.

17

And Bill had told him all about it. Malcolm began pacing again, jauntily and confidently, contemptuous of her calm, bored eyes, because he knew now that the words would flow like oil from his lips. "Once upon a time—" He paused and smiled condescendingly at her. "This is a classic story, with a classic beginning, you see. Once upon a time I knew a girl. Many years ago in New York. She was young and lovely and, appropriately enough, she placed a very high value on her youth and loveliness. She was one of those creatures who make you doubt both the wisdom and kindness of God. She was so flawless, so beautiful, that when she walked the streets of the city she made all those who were old and ill-favored realize that they had been cruelly cheated by life. And I knew her, Tani," Malcolm said, his voice rising with excitement. "Not significantly, not intimately—" he dismissed the notion with a large wave of his hand "—but she allowed me to take her to dinner, to drive her to various appointments —she was a model, you see, for fashion magazines. I was one of a dozen young men who served her as faithful supplicants." But this hadn't happened to him at all, Malcolm thought apprehensively. He risked a glance at Tani. Would she know he was lying? That this wasn't his story, that it belonged to someone named Bill Harvey? To his dismay, he saw the wings of her nostrils flare with a yawn. "Now I'm coming to the choice part," he cried, and began to speak so rapidly that the words were twisted into strange awkward shapes as they tumbled from his mouth. "Here's the part that's full of irony and sight gags and pratfalls. Her name was Karen. Did I mention that? And she owned Toto, the French poodle. So I cunningly decided to make a friend of Toto, to creep into his savage little heart. But this wasn't easy. Toto was moody and selfish, and he, too, placed an extremely high value on himself, a notion he had picked up from his mistress. So I laid my plans carefully. I found a butcher to cut me bite-sized cubes of the finest fillet of beef, and I wrapped these in cellophane and brought one or two with me each time I called on Karen. Victory was not immediate. The little bastard would have nothing to do with me at first. It snarled at me, it bared its needle-sharp fangs as if it wanted a bite out of me instead of the choice tidbits I was coaxing him to eat. But I was patient, and I wore him down. Finally we became fast friends. It was touching; he sat in my lap, trotted at my heels, and stood with his little paws on the window sill looking down into Park Avenue for a glimpse of my yellow convertible. We were a thing, an item, a living testament to love and devotion." He was so confident now that he paused for effect, and smiled at Tani. "Do you find this entertaining so far?"

"Please finish it quickly," she said, and there was such coldness in her voice that a tremor of fear shook his body.

"Yes, yes, I'm coming to the funny part now," he said pleadingly, "You must listen. I loved Karen, and I asked her to marry me." Suddenly, blessedly, all of his thoughts fused together in a clear and lucid pattern, and he knew that the comfort and relief of alcohol was almost within his hands. He remembered in vivid detail the night Bill Harvey had returned to the apartment they shared, to tell him that he had proposed to Karen. That had been in the summertime, seven, eight, nine years ago, before the Third Avenue El had been torn down, and even now Malcolm could remember the roaring crash of the trains that had punctured Bill Harvey's long, comical recital of the end of his affair with Karen. "Yes, I asked her to marry me," Malcolm said, seating himself impulsively on the footstool before Tani's chair. "I loved her enough to marry her, so this is not only a very funny story, but a very serious one, too. She said to me, as girls will, 'This is such a surprise, I had no idea you felt this way. I must have time to think it over.' She thought about it for a week," Malcolm said, studying Tani's expressionless face hopefully, praying for a ripple of interest to break its smooth surface, or a glint of amusement to lighten her dark, liquid eyes. Then he plunged on. "When the week was up, I hurried around to her apartment for the verdict. But she was gone, Tani! The manager of the building told me she had gone to Florida for the winter. But there was a note for me. There's always a note, you know. In her charming, childish handwriting, Karen told me that she didn't love me. She was sorry, she wished she could love me, but the fact was she just plain didn't. But she liked and respected me, she appreciated my companionship and devotion, and, as proof of this, she had decided to leave a token of her esteem for me. Something which I had obviously loved almost as much as I had loved her—" Malcolm laughed exuberantly and poked Tani's knee with his forefinger in a confident, intimate gesture which urged her to join him in this vast joke.

"Can't you guess it?" he said, twisting his mouth until it stretched in a tight, straining smile. "She left me her dog! She left me Toto!" Malcolm threw back his head and laughed until he could hear the sound crashing wildly and erratically from the walls of the small room. He stood and paced the floor, shoulders heaving with spasmodic laughter. "Isn't that magnificent? Isn't that hilarious?" He stopped and stared at her, suddenly fearful of her silence, her cool and faintly contemptuous expression. "Isn't it funny?" he said tentatively; his confidence was gone and a sullen, uneasy anger burned in him now. "Well, don't you get it?" he said, in a harsh, strident voice, trying to bully her into a conciliatory mood. "Don't you get the joke?"

"Go away from here," she said.

"No, no," Malcolm said, shaking his head desperately. The words that came from his throat were like a hideous little moan. "Don't say that, please. It's funny, Tani. I know it is. It's amusing. Please smile." He dropped to his knees before her in an attitude of helpless supplication. "Please smile, Tani. Please."

"You are drunk and you are stupid," she said. "Get out now."

"It's not fair, it isn't fair at all," Malcolm said. He felt victimized and betrayed; he had done his best, he thought sullenly. As he got to his feet, the anger in him grew hotly and dangerously. "Goddamit, laugh, you whore," he said, shouting the words at her. "I'll make you laugh. You don't want jokes. You want a man to rip his guts out and throw his filth at your feet. That's the only thing that would make you smile. You want misery, pain, terror. I can give you all you want. Listen: seven months ago my wife was killed." Malcolm spat out the words as if they were hot coals on his tongue. "She was decent and kind and lovely. But she died in a flaming coffin seven months ago. She left me, do you hear? She left me on this stupid, meaningless earth. She left me all alone."

Malcolm put a hand against the wall to steady himself; a pain beyond enduring grew as the pale face of his dead wife shone as still and quiet as a star in his mind. "She left me forever," he said in a straining voice. "She's gone and I can find no one to replace her if I searched the world for eternity. I am alone, and I'll never find her again."

Tani laughed softly. "That's much better. That's very funny."

Malcolm stared incredulously at her, convinced that his mind had finally broken under the burden of pain. This wasn't happening, this wasn't real; in a thousand heavens and hells no one would laugh at his agony.

But it was true, it was real, for Tani was smiling at him, and her eyes were bubbling with excitement and mirth. And as he stared at her, shaking his head like someone hurt beyond his capacity to bear it, Tani laughed at him and said, "Yes, you are being very funny now. Can you tell me more stories like that?"

"It's true, damn you. it's true," Malcolm said hoarsely. "My wife is dead. Her plane crashed in the sea. Do you think I'm making it up?"

"No, I'm sure it's true," Tani said. "That's why it's so funny. You are sad because you are left all alone. You are weeping for yourself because you are alone and have lost a toy. You don't weep for her, who is dead and whose future life can never happen. You are crying for yourself. You are being honest, and it's always funny when men are honest."

Malcolm lunged across the ottoman, his fingers clawing for her slim throat. In his fury, he wanted the feel of her neck in his hands: he wanted to tighten them until her derisive eyes were lifeless as stones, and the blasphemous words were dead forever on her swollen tongue. But he stumbled weakly across her languid legs, and would have pitched to the floor except for the powerful hands which caught him and pushed him roughly toward the door.

"Don't hurt him, Jorge," Tani said. "He did make me smile, after all."

Jorge opened the door, placed a foot in the small of Malcolm's back and kicked him through the doorway into the street.

Malcolm felt a rush of air on his face, stones stinging his hands and knees, and finally a trickle of slime running down the gutter against his face. He lay in the sunlight of a new day with flies gathering about his dark head, while the furies within him sheathed their claws, folded their wings, and waited for him to wake.

3

THE police constable of Cartama was a middle-aged man named Don Fernando Gonzalez, and he wore a gray twill uniform with red collar tabs, and a holstered automatic on his black belt.

As a boy he had dreamed of two things: to become police chief of the village he had been born in, and to earn enough money to enjoy the classic Spanish Sunday of a late Mass, a leisurely lunch of *paella* and white wine, and then the bullfights in Málaga with enough pesetas left over to provide sherry and cigars for the night's discussion of the *corrida*. His father had been a gardener at the villa of a wealthy family from Madrid who spent their summers on the coast near Cartama. Their support and interest had encouraged Fernando to complete his elementary schooling, and this had made him eligible for the Civil Service. He had chosen the department of police, and inevitably—or so it seemed to him now—he had become the constable of Cartama.

The other dream, however, still eluded him, and he was thinking of this rather gloomily as he rode along the sunny coastal road on the bus to Málaga. He could afford the lunch of *paella* and white wine on Sundays, but bullfight tickets had been driven out of his reach by the tourists. As he looked out the window of the bus at the thick cluster of villas and bars and hotels which had sprouted along the coast in the past few years, he remembered the old days, when the few wealthy men of the village had come down from their *fincas* in black suits for the Sunday bullfights in Málaga. The heat, the dust, the smells of wine and shrimps mingling with the rank fumes of their old cars had been an intoxicating fragrance to Fernando. As a boy he had longed to be part of this; to talk wisely of crops and weather with his friends over sherry and *puros,* and then to drive sedately to the bull ring, where he would take his cushioned seat in the shade after raising a hat to the President's box and exchanging greetings with friends in their places at the *barrera.* Now it seemed to Don Fernando that he was no closer to realizing that dream than he had been as a round-eyed child standing barefoot in the dust of his village.

In Málaga Don Fernando walked along the wide, palm-shaded boulevard which flanked the city's harbor until he came to the low office building where the Great Seal of the United States gleamed in the sun, and an American flag fluttered in the stiff, warm breezes off the sea. Brushing a speck of dust from the shoulder of his tunic, Don Fernando entered the cool lobby.

Five minuted later he was explaining his mission to an American named Peter Kelly, who was his country's representative in Málaga. Kelly was in his early thirties, but in spite of his youth, his untidy red hair and tall, gangling frame, there was a quietness in his manner, a certain dignity and formality, which pleased and soothed Don Fernando. After accepting a cigarette, Don Fernando got down to business. He spoke in Spanish.

"He has done nothing wrong, but he is always drunk, and he is a bad example to the village. This morning he was found unconscious in an alley in the Arroyo de Miel. Naturally, we put him in jail. He has no money, no clothing, no place to stay. He may sleep on the beach, there is no law against it, but I cannot allow him to become a public charge. I do not know what is to be done. We will release him when he is sober, but that is no solution. Do you know if he has family or friends?"

"I imagine he has friends," Kelly said. "But I'm not sure they'd be able to help him. Tell me, Don Fernando, do you know anything about Tony Malcolm?"

"Nothing at all."

"He and his wife were well-known photographers and writers. They worked for the important magazines, *Life, Paris-Match, Reálités, Holiday,* and so forth. Malcolm took the pictures, and his wife did the text. They were talented people, and their approach was always odd and unusual. I remember a piece they did on the expatriate American colony in Paris a few years ago. It was from the viewpoint of a waiter, what he saw and heard and what he served the American beatniks and so forth. Hardly a routine slant, you see."

Don Fernando nodded politely. "Most original."

"I've pieced together some of Malcolm's background," Kelly said. "When I learned he was stopping here, I made it my business to. For a year or so, he was drinking pretty heavily. One of his friends told me it wasn't disastrous—he just loved a good time. But it was beginning to interfere with his work. He'd miss assignments occasionally, or arrive too late for pictures. Things like that. Meanwhile his wife, Jane, covered for him; she was a photographer, too, not in Malcolm's class, but if he were too drunk, or too hung over, to work, she could handle both ends of the assignment. Early this year Malcolm was scheduled to fly to Dakar alone to cover a story for a British magazine. He and his wife were in Barcelona at the time and apparently Malcolm got on a week-end binge with some friends of his, and came down with pneumonia. He couldn't make the trip. His wife put him in a hospital, made sure he was being well taken care of, and then took his tickets

23

and caught the plane to Dakar." Kelly sighed faintly. "You may remember. The pilot asked for a routine fix an hour out of Dakar. That was the last word from him. The plane went down in the sea, and there were no survivors."

"A tragedy," Don Fernando said. "And this happened early in the year, is that correct?" ·

"Yes, nearly seven months ago."

"She was a handsome woman?"

"Very lovely, I believe, and very young."

"He believes he killed her, of course."

"He's been on a collision course with oblivion ever since it happened."

Don Fernando stared out the windows at the harbor. He could see gulls wheeling against the sky, freighters lined up like squat suckling animals at the sides of the dock. Lowering his gaze he studied the tall statue of General Marques de Larios, which gives the main avenue of Málaga its name.

"It's a pity he doesn't believe in God," he said at last.

"You mean, there'd be someone for him to love?"

Don Fernando shrugged. "Or someone to hate."

"What do you plan to do?"

"I will need a letter from you to support the fact that I have brought the matter to your attention. Only for my files. That is important. Sometimes what is written down in the files is more important than what eventually happens. Beyond that I can think of nothing more to do just now. . . ."

Malcolm was released from jail that afternoon. The guard, a man named Henrique, gave him a plate of cold fish, some rice, and a glass of wine, before unlocking the door of his cell and turning him out into the streets. Malcolm had no recollection of how he spent the rest of the day. He started to walk to Torremolinos, nine miles up the coast, for he remembered a man who was staying there, a French magazine editor, who might give him some money. But after a few hundred yards he stopped and sat on a rock beside the road. At dusk he was picked up by three young men in a car. They drove him back to Cartama. One of them was called Jeff by his friends, and he gave Malcolm a drink from a bottle of brandy.

The wind off the sea was turning cold, and the sun had dropped from sight when Malcolm began the long trip up the twisting road to the Arroyo de Miel. He had decided to go to Domingo's. It was miles above him in the darkness, but he knew he would get there somehow; and in his weary mind was the conviction that this would solve all his problems.

He was almost sober now, and sick with the pain of his memories. Each step forward was a victory that might never be equalled again, but his eyes were blazing with unreasoning hope, for he sensed that he was struggling slowly and steadily toward a final release, and that his miserable journey along the brink of guilt and despair might be coming to an end at last.

4

DOMINGO'S was crowded that night, with fishermen pressed close together along the bar and waiters working quickly to serve the groups seated at tables. The first thing a stranger might have noticed was the silence; the waiters moved about as softly as cats, and the bartender, an old man named Pepe, tended to his customers with an almost priestlike gravity. There was no clatter of bottles or glasses, no ring of coins on the bar, and the fishermen, like devout acolytes, reflected the bartender's mood in their solemn expressions and hushed voices.

In the middle of the large, square room stood a poker table with a green felt cover shining under a naked overhead light bulb. It was the most prominent feature in Domingo's bar: this large round table, and the inevitable group of players sitting about it, their faces sharply etched by the naked light beating down on them from the low, beamed ceiling.

From this table radiated the mood of the evening; it was like a heartbeat pounding slowly and steadily beneath the life of the room, regulating and dominating the reactions of everyone present. Strangers quickly adjusted themselves to these currents of excitement and fear and anger which eddied from the game and dictated the emotional tone of Domingo's bar.

For when Domingo was winning everyone was happy, and the smoky air trembled with noise and laughter. When he lost the room became still and quiet, and tonight he was losing; and so the piano was silent; the musician stood with the fishermen at the bar, while Tani sat alone at her table turning the pages of a magazine so slowly and carefully that the sound was only a whisper on the air. She wore a white silk dress, high heels, and a twist of jasmine in her hair, but the festivity of her costume mocked the look in her eyes as she risked a cautious glance at Domingo, whose luck was running very badly that night.

Domingo was a Frenchman who had come to Spain near the end of the war with Germany. That much was definitely known about him, but the details of his background were obscure; some said he had deserted from the French army, others that he had collaborated with the German Occupation and had fled to escape reprisals from the Maquis. Whatever the facts, he had lived on the southern shores of Spain ever since, settling himself firmly and comfortably into his bar and villa above the hills of Cartama. He was a huge and powerful man, with small, alert eyes which glittered softly and watchfully over the hard rolls of flesh which bulged above the fringe of his black beard. Tales of his prodigious strength were told up and down the coast. He had once collapsed a horse with only the pressure of his knees against its ribs. He could snap a quarter-inch rope as other men would a shoe-string. Inevitably, when a small and tattered circus had come to the village one summer, Domingo had delighted his admirers by hoisting the circus strongman and one of his heaviest weights above his head.

He was known to be brutal with women, and it was rumored that his bar was only a front for his real occupation, which was smuggling cigarettes, coffee, and whiskey into Spain from somewhere in Africa. But in the welter of guesses and gossip which surrounded the huge Frenchman, there was one fact no one disputed: that was the anger which infected him like a disease when he was losing at cards.

The three men playing with Domingo that night avoided his eyes; they flipped out their cards without studying them, and there was a certain desperation in their manner, as if they hoped that the rapidity of the play might hasten the end of the game. They were like men in a locked room listening to the faint sounds of a ticking bomb.

On Domingo's right was an Englishman named Clarke, who wore a blazer with a silk scarf knotted loosely under the open collar of his soiled white shirt. He had gray hair, gray eyes, gray skin, and a smile that flickered like quicksilver on his dry lips. In spite of the expression of cautious cruelty in his eyes, there was something both wistful and guarded about him, as if he might be remembering a good deed done long ago, while steeling himself to make sure no such lapse occurred again.

Opposite Domingo sat a Pole named Zarren, a squat, middle-aged man with a bald head and neatly trimmed blond mustaches. Everything about him suggested the woebegone, from the shabbiness of his clothes to the sadly resigned gaze he was presently directing at the cards in his blunt fingers.

To Domingo's left was a young man named Paco. He had glossy black hair, tenderly arranged in swooping waves, large, liquid brown eyes, and smooth, rosy-brown skin, and this combination of assets had led him into a series of profitable relationships with female tourists up and down the coast. Paco had been born to be a fisherman like his father, but the maturity of his tall, well-muscled body had coincided with the tourist boom in Spain, and instead of becoming a fisherman, as God and his father had ordained, Paco had become a gigolo.

As a result he owned a silver wrist watch, a silver cigarette case, a colorful wardrobe, and a small, shiny motorcycle. Paco was supremely confident at this moment in life that the world had been created solely for his own physical enjoyment. In Cartama, at this very hour, a blonde American woman with wide, hospitable hips was waiting for him, and after he had given her the privilege of going to bed with him, they would go dancing at a smart club in Torremolinos, where he would drink whiskey and enjoy the music and meet still more pretty tourists. It was so fine to be young and handsome, he was thinking, and he was so full of contentment with himself that he committed the indiscretion of patting Domingo on the shoulder.

"Not your lucky night, eh?" he said smiling.

Domingo slapped Paco's hand away with stinging force. "Don't talk, play cards," he said.

"Yes, of course," Paco said hastily.

"You have someone to meet?" Domingo said, staring at him closely.

"It doesn't matter. It's not important. I can meet her after the game."

"After the game, remember that," Domingo said.

"*Claro, claro,*" Paco said and grinned nervously as he turned away from the heat and anger in Domingo's eyes.

The cards continued to flash about under the strong light, and the tension in the room increased as Domingo lost pot

27

after pot, until finally only a handful of coins glittered before him on the green felt table. Zarren and Clarke and Paco were desperately trying to lose now; they were afraid of winning any more from Domingo, but in spite of their deliberate inattention and deliberate mistakes, nothing seemed able to dam or deflect the steady, downhill flow of the Frenchman's luck.

Clarke said cautiously, "Might be useful to take a breather. Change the run of the bloody cards, eh?"

"Deal!" Domingo said, rapping a fist softly on the table. And the cards continued to spin.

Malcolm was exhausted when he finally reached the Arroyo de Miel. Weakness and fear had hounded him close to delirium, but when he saw the lights of Domingo's bar shining through the darkness, his strength returned in a last, flaring burst and he stumbled on toward the life promised by the pale yellow lights in the windows of the bar.

Somehow he knew this was his last chance; he could afford no mistake, no miscalculation. In the darkness outside Domingo's, he rested an instant, gathering all that was left of his wits and strength for a final challenge. He must be clever and casual, of course; his voice and hands mustn't betray his needs; he must tell his story calmly and clearly, but with an authority that would preclude the possibility of anyone's doubting it. He told himself these things, fiercely and tensely, while willing his hands to stop trembling and trying to relax the lines of fear and anxiety in his face.

At last he squared his shoulders, brushed the dirty strands of hair from his forehead, and pushed open the door of the bar.

He was surprised and gratified by the silence in the room. Noise might have confused him, but everything was blessedly still and quiet. The fishermen were silent, the piano was silent, even the men at the poker table were silent. This increased his confidence. It was an encouraging atmosphere, an appropriate atmosphere in which to reveal his good news. He wouldn't need to raise his voice to be heard, and that was fitting and fortunate, for he wanted an attentive audience, a thoughtful audience, one gracious enough to listen to his good fortune in a respectful silence.

Malcolm found a place for himself at the end of the bar. Domingo's was pleasant, he thought; very quiet, very well run, and larger than he had remembered it. The walls stretched away forever, shining with lovely lights, an infinity of distance to encompass an infinity of silence. The thought made him dizzy, and he put his hands quickly against the bar to steady himself. Malcolm wondered with some confusion why he had gone to the trouble of making up a story for this quiet and respectful audience. The truth was so much more exciting. He realized with relief that there was no need to lie any more.

Everything had worked out fine. He didn't remember exactly where he had got the good news, and he wasn't certain of the details, but he knew if he just stood quietly in this silent shining room everything would be all right.

Pepe was watching him impassively.

"Good evening," Malcolm said. He wondered how long Pepe had been standing there; Malcolm had been sure he was alone in the room. "You're looking very well, Pepe." Malcolm felt superior and indulgent. Pepe was all right, he thought a good man.

Pepe nodded expressionlessly.

Malcolm rubbed a hand over his heavy growth of whiskers and winked slyly at him. "I don't look very well, do I?"

Pepe shrugged slightly but said nothing.

"Let me tell you something," Malcolm said, winking again at Pepe. He leaned closer to the old man. "I've had a real stroke of luck. One of the biggest magazines in America sent me a cable today. They want me to do a series of stories on the southern coast of Spain. The bullfights, flamenco dancing, the tourist boom, the works. It's the greatest assignment I've ever had in my life. I feel like the luckiest guy in the world. Quite frankly, congratulations are in order."

As Malcolm finished speaking the room erupted with cheerful, relaxed laughter and the musician hurried from the bar to his piano. Everyone was draining or filling a glass, and the talk and laughter and music bouncing about the room sounded relieved and happy.

Malcolm's smile was puzzled but grateful; it was odd, such applause and approval in this shining empty place, but he knew the audience was there, understanding and sharing his good fortune. They would do the story together, of course; he could imagine Janey's surprise at the news, imagine her coming off a plane with the wind tossing her blonde hair about, hurrying to him on those adorable skinny legs of hers, and her smiling face as excited as a flag flying in a high wind.

They knew all the ins and outs of Europe, the best beaches, the best ski slopes, the warm and comfortable hotels in Paris and Zurich where you found the bars full of the same pleasant people you had just left in Madrid or Copenhagen or Barcelona. . . .

He tightened his hands on the bar, feeling the sudden, uneven stroke of his heart.

Pepe shouldn't have left him all alone, he realized; he was too shaken by his good fortune to be left alone. But Pepe was busy serving drinks to the laughing fishermen at the bar, and Malcolm waited patiently for him to return so that he could tell him the rest of his good news. After that he and Pepe would have a few drinks together to celebrate; yes, definitely a few drinks, and definitely with Pepe, for he was a good man and Malcolm wanted to share his happiness with him. But some instinct warned him not to tell anyone else. No, he would stand here quietly, ignoring the laughter around him, and wait for Pepe. And he mustn't cry. No one would understand that he was weeping simply because everything had turned out all right. . . .

Domingo had won two hands in a row, and the change in his mood had generated a tense and happy excitement in the barroom. He was laughing exuberantly. The hard rolls of flesh above his beard squeezed his eyes so deeply into their sockets that they were only glittering points of light in his huge face. The piano player's fingers flashed nimbly over the keys of the old upright, making strident music in praise of Domingo, and Tani stood and strolled into the bright arc of light cast by the bulb above the poker table. She smiled at Domingo's cards. The glaring illumination from the naked bulb gleamed on her white dress, sparkled in her black hair, and lay in gentle golden patterns on her bare arms and legs. Like a slender lightning rod, she seemed to draw all illumination and excitement in the room about her white figure.

Domingo raised, then raised again, and his laughter boomed against the walls of the room like the roar of an animal.

The sound confused Malcolm; it shattered his moment of peace. This was a bar, he realized, and he had come here to get something to drink. He felt fear in his throat and the need for liquor burning inside like a hot poker. The booming laughter had subsided abruptly, and he was grateful for that, but the same voice was cursing at something now in a tone of outraged bitterness.

Malcolm waved desperately to Pepe, and when the old man came over to him, he said, "It's all true, everything I told you. They're sending me travellers' checks, and a bank draft. I'll get my cameras back, and all my luggage." But he knew he was lying, and the knowledge drained him of all his strength. There was no job, nothing but the need for oblivion. He tried to laugh, but tears stung his cheeks. "I need a drink, Pepe," he said weakly. "Please don't say no. I've got to have a drink."

Pepe leaned cautiously toward Malcolm. "Go away, don't make trouble," he said. "I can't give you anything to drink." He nodded toward the men at the poker table. "Domingo has said no. I cannot do what he tells me not to."

"Please," Malcolm said. "Please."

"I cannot, I am sorry," Pepe said, and his eyes were sad, but not for Christ himself would he have poured a drink against Domingo's orders.

"Deal the cards!" Domingo was shouting. The palm of his hand struck the table with the sound of a pistol shot, and a ten peseta coin bounced at the impact and fell to the floor, where it rolled about in a little circle before tipping over and rattling to a stop on its side.

Zarren quickly dealt out the cards. Malcolm found himself staring at the coin on the floor. It had a hypnotic effect on him; it seemed to be winking suggestively at him. He rubbed his eyes and felt the tears on his hand. The coin looked friendly and inviting, shining innocently under the bright light.

Malcolm straightened himself with an effort. He walked unsteadily toward the glittering coin, unaware of Pepe's harshly whispered warning, or the plucking fingers of a fisherman who tried to pull him back to the bar.

He knelt on the floor and picked up the coin with trembling fingers. The silence stretched tightly through the room as he held out his hand to Domingo, the coin shining purely, but somehow disdainfully, against the skin of his open palm. Everyone looked quickly away from Malcolm; no one wanted to be involved, even as a spectator, in this business. The fishermen intently studied their wine glasses, and Pepe turned his back on the poker table and stared with a completely neutral expression at the rows of bottles behind the bar. Tani backed slowly out of the arc light enveloping the gamblers, and sat at her own table, crossing her legs and looking carefully at the backs of her small hands.

In the thick, smothering silence, Malcolm's voice sounded almost blasphemous. He said, "Please, may I have this? Please? For a drink?"

Domingo turned his huge head slowly and stared at Malcolm, as if he couldn't quite believe what he was seeing; he seemed perplexed by this filthy bearded creature at his

31

feet, this grotesque apparition who knelt before him in an attitude of haggard supplication. Finally he shrugged and looked blankly at Clarke and Paco and Zarren, as if they might provide some explanation for this preposterous situation. He seemed genuinely puzzled by Malcolm's incredible presumption, and too stunned for a moment to do anything about it.

"Please, it's only ten pesetas," Malcolm said, whispering the words helplessly. "Please."

Domingo's honest bewilderment was replaced by an anger which seemed to consume him like a swiftly spurting fire. He caught Malcolm's shoulder in one huge hand, and jerked him close to him. With the other he snatched the coin from his trembling fingers.

"You pig, you rotten pig," he said, in a voice that shook with the need for violence. "You drunk, you filthy drunk, I wouldn't pay ten pesetas to watch you shoot yourself."

With an almost careless sweep of his arm, he flung Malcolm aside, and then he turned back to the poker table. still burning with anger. "All right, play the cards," he said, while his hot eyes searched the faces of Clarke and Paco and Zarren. "Maybe you think it's funny? Goddamit, then laugh! Go on! Let me hear you laugh!"

There was no sound at all as Clarke hastily dealt out the cards. Malcolm lay on the cold floor. Directly in line with his eyes, he saw a small red bug. It moved along slowly but steadily, triumphing over match sticks and shrimp husks like a sturdy little tank. Malcolm watched the red bug until it disappeared among the bare feet of the fishermen standing at the bar.

He was breathing quietly and evenly. The deep lines of pain and desperation faded gradually from his face, until finally his expression became as cold and unrevealing as a death mask. There was no anodyne waiting for him here, or anywhere else in the world. He knew that now. There was no longer a cheap and fleeting oblivion available to him; and he realized, numbly and gratefully, that he had come at last to the end of his long, agonizing journey.

Malcolm raised himself to his knees.

"Domingo, listen to me," he said, and there was something new in his voice then, a certain weary indifference, which caused the big Frenchman to turn and regard him with a puzzled frown.

"You want another lesson?" Domingo said at last.

"No, I've had my lesson," Malcolm said. "I only want you to

listen. You said you wouldn't pay ten pesetas to watch me shoot myself." He smiled faintly. "How much will you pay?"

"You're crazy," Domingo said, but after rubbing a hand over his mouth he put his cards down and shifted about in his chair to face Malcolm. "You must be crazy," he said slowly.

"No, I'm not crazy," Malcolm said. "I only want to make a bargain with you. I agree that ten pesetas is probably too high. It's exorbitant, in fact. So let's try to find a fair price. Every human action must be worth something. How much is it worth to you? Eight pesetas? Five pesetas?" He laughed weakly at the excitement he could see in Domingo's narrowing. eyes "Come on, make me an offer. It's got to be worth something."

The mood of the poker table had become uneasy.

"I think we should play our cards," Clarke said.

"No, wait," Domingo said, looking intensely at Malcolm. "You're not crazy? But you'll kill yourself for a few pesetas?"

Malcolm closed his eyes and nodded his head slowly. He felt nothing but relief, a blessed sense of impending peace, at this opportunity to put down the pointless, weary burden of his life.

"All right, I'll make you an offer," Domingo said. He paused to take a cigar from his pocket, light it, and flip the match aside carelessly. Then he said, "It's worth a glass of wine to me. One glass of wine."

"Make it brandy."

"All right then, brandy."

"You've got a deal," Malcolm said.

Domingo smiled slowly. "You're nothing, you know it? You're less than the bugs on the floor. You're worthless."

"No, I'm worth a glass of brandy."

Domingo's smile grew wider then, for this game appealed to him very much; he hated dignity and self-respect in other men, and the spectacle of Malcolm on his knees begging to throw his life away filled him with excitement. A cold, pleasurable pressure grew in his stomach, as he reached into his pocket and drew out a small revolver.

"Let's be sure we understand each other," he said, and placed the gun on the table with the butt-plate pointing toward Malcolm. "I don't make deals for fun," he said, his voice falling softly across the silence in the room. Everyone in the bar stared in fascination at the gun. It was small and ugly against the green felt of the table, and the harsh overhead light flickered like tiny fires along the blue barrel and black hand-grips. It didn't look ominous or dangerous; it didn't bring the feel of death into the room; it was simply businesslike and functional, a specific tool for a specific job, and this gave its presence a grotesque, matter-of-fact kind of horror.

"All right, I'll buy you a glass of brandy," Domingo said. "That's my end of the bargain. Then you pick up this gun and shoot yourself. You understand? Is it clear?"

"Yes," Malcolm said, in a thick, empty voice but a smile touched his lips as he heard Domingo tell Pepe to bring a glass of Fundador to the table. He knew now that he had a price, a value. All of his dreams and hopes, the conviction he shared with all mankind that there had been something significant and eternal glowing inside this lump of clay—all of that in the truth of time was worth only a small glass of brandy.

Pepe placed the brandy on the poker table, and returned hastily to his place behind the bar.

"Enjoy it," Domingo said. "It will be your last drink."

Malcolm cupped the glass in his hands and brought it slowly to his lips, still kneeling before Domingo like a votary in the presence of a gross idol. He didn't feel the liquor on his lips or throat, but when it struck his stomach it spread warmly through his body, filling him with the unwelcome promise of strength and life.

When he replaced the empty glass on the wooden rim of the table, the faint click was like a thunderclap in the silent room. Domingo nodded deliberately toward the small gun.

"Now you owe me for the drink," he said.

Clarke laughed nervously. "It's a good joke, at that. Shows how far down hill a chap can slide, doesn't it?" His voice was dry as bone.

"Now we finish our game," Zarren said, peering through the smoke at Domingo. "All right? We play cards?"

"Shut up," Domingo said. He stared intently at Malcolm. "I told you I don't make deals for fun. You try to trick me out of a drink, I'll teach you some other tricks."

Malcolm picked up the gun and got slowly to his feet. "Don't worry," he said.

Paco ran trembling hands across his thick lustrous black hair, and then locked them tightly together between his knees. He tried not to look at Malcolm or Domingo; his eyes rolled about in his head like those of a frightened horse.

Malcolm frowned at the gun, and then, quite deliberately, he placed the muzzle against his temple.

Zarren said quickly, "Don't let him do this, Domingo. I warn you."

Tani leaped to her feet and ran to Domingo's side, her high heels clattering with a sound of panic through the silence. She shook Domingo's beefy arm. "You fool, you fool," she said. "He's going to do it. He's not joking. He's going to do it."

Domingo disengaged her hands with a mere twitch of his shoulder, but the force of it caused her to stagger as if she had been brushed by a charging bull.

"Shoot!" Domingo said, his voice trembling with excitement.

Malcolm closed his eyes and pulled the trigger. The sound of the shot rocked through the room, and Tani screamed as Malcolm dropped to his knees, his head rolling limply on his shoulders. . . .

Later there were interminable discussions about what had actually happened; but the only logical reconstruction was that Domingo had been watching Malcolm's slowly whitening knuckle, and had—at that instant the trigger was pulled—slapped the gun away from his temple. The bullet had gone through Malcolm's hair, furrowing his scalp lightly, and digging itself into a beam above the bar. Later, Domingo had the bullet removed, drilled a hole through it, and wore it on his watch chain.

Malcolm sat on the floor, his weight supported with one hand, sobbing softly and helplessly. Paco stood abruptly and ran from the room and those inside could hear him vomiting in the street. Only Domingo seemed to look at Malcolm. Zarren and Clarke stared at the top of the poker table, and the fishermen stood with their backs to him, shoulders hunched defensively, as if there was something menacing in the sound of his weak sobs. Tani sat at her table and rubbed the tips of her fingers slowly against her temples.

But Domingo seemed clinically interested in this matter. He studied the physical evidence of Malcolm's degradation with greedy eyes, as if he were making an effort to calculate and analyze the precise amount of shame represented by the slack curve of his body, the listless droop of his head, the weak noises sounding in his throat.

Then he turned and spoke to the fishermen, who nodded quickly, gulped down their drinks and filed out the door. When the last of them had gone, Domingo looked at Zarren and Clarke.

"Get him out of here," he said, nodding at Malcolm. "Take

35

him to the village. Put him in a good room. Give him whatever he wants to drink. If he sleeps, stay with him until he wakes."

"No, it's not good," Zarren said. "It's bad to destory a man and let him live."

"I don't like it," Clarke said savagely. "What bloody use is he now? It's what happens to a man if you flog him hard enough and long enough. Chuck him into the street and forget him."

"No, you're both wrong," Domingo said, looking fondly at Malcolm's huddled figure. "You don't understand." He put his large hands on the poker table, and leaned forward until his face was only inches from Zarren's and Clarke's. He was smiling, and his eyes were shining with secret amusement.

"For one glass of brandy he will kill himself," Domingo said softly. "For a whole bottle, he might kill anyone we tell him to. Someone who needs killing, eh?" Domingo chuckled and patted their shoulders. "Do you understand now?"

"I don't like it," Clarke said.

"Do what I tell you," Domingo said, and the swiftly growing anger in his voice was like a sharp prod under Clarke and Zarren. They stood quickly, and half-carried, half-dragged Malcolm through the door.

Domingo strolled over to the bar. There was a lingering smile on his face, like that of a man who had just finished an excellent dinner with a bottle of wine, and now was speculating on what other pleasures he might expect from the evening.

"Do you wish something?" Pepe asked him.

Domingo laughed and took a ten peseta coin from his pocket, the one he had snatched from Malcolm's trembling hand. "Yes, give me a brandy," he said, and tossed the coin onto the bar.

5

THE following morning Don Fernando, the policeman, rode up to the Arroyo de Miel on his bicycle. It was a clear and pleasant day, and the flowers along the narrow road gleamed vividly in the dry air. He rapped briskly on Tani's door, and Jorge let him in. Don Fernando stood at the window of her living room, admiring the early sunlight on the sea. When she came into the room, he turned and smiled briefly at her.

"You're very pale," he said. "Are you all right?"

"I didn't sleep well," she said, and sat listless in the deep chair. She wore her customary daytime costume of blue jeans, and a white shirt, but there was no necklace at her throat, no bracelets on her wrists. Shadows like purple bruises lay under her eyes, and her thick black hair fell loosely to her shoulders. "I'm glad it's nothing serious," Don Fernando said. He drew a leather-bound notebook from one pocket of his tunic, a fountain pen from another, and said cripsly, "What do you have to tell me this morning?"

"There isn't much." She was silent a moment, her face pensive and thoughtful within its frame of heavy, dark hair. "There was a man who came here a week or so ago, a very young man. He said Spain was dirty. He said all the people were thieves."

"Good," Don Fernando said, and began writing quickly in his notebook.

"He called Franco many bad names."

"Excellent," Don Fernando said. "An American?"

"I think so."

"You have his name?"

"No."

"His description?"

"He was young, with red hair. He wore khaki pants and a white shirt."

"Very well," Don Fernando said cheerfully and continued to make rapid notes in his book. "Is there anything else?"

"No, nothing."

"That's quite all right. You mustn't be discouraged."

Don Fernando used Tani as an informer for reasons which had very little to do with his job of keeping the peace in Cartama. He used Tani, and the information she supplied him, as a potential political parachute. The gossip and rumors she collected were kept faithfully in his notebooks, and he knew there was a chance that these neat little archives might someday save his life.

Don Fernando had lived through one Civil War by having accidentally chosen the winning side. It was only a matter of luck that he hadn't been pulled from his bed and shot in the streets, and he didn't intend to leave such an important matter to chance again. Not that it mattered to him which groups or forces led the government—call them red, blue or green, it made no difference at all to Don Fernando. What mattered was safety, and the trick about being safe was to acquire the chameleon's art of blending invisibly into the colors that surrounded it. And the colors Don Fernando hoped to lose himself against were the colors of strength and victory.

Now there were dangerous currents stirring in the country. Priests talking against the government, miners striking, students marching in various protests, bombs breaking the peace of the large cities.

Don Fernando took no action at all on the information Tani gave him. This was the subtle strength of his plan. If the present government continued in force, he could point to his collection of notebooks, crammed with their accounts of subversive hearsay, as evidence that he had been loyally ferreting out its detractors and enemies. But since he took no action, made no arrests, he would be able to prove to a rebel force that he had done nothing at all to help the government.

Perhaps this wouldn't be enough; but he intended to have something to say in his defense when and if the knocking sounded on his door late in the night.

Don Fernando had come to have a superstitious feeling about Tani. As long as she stayed in the village he believed himself to be safe. It was blasphemy, he realized, to regard a whore as a patron saint, but Don Fernando had the uneasy fear that this was precisely how he felt about Tani.

As he was putting his notebook away, she said abruptly, "I want to go away. Can't I go away?"

"There are entries in your passport which are irregular. I must study them carefully."

"You've had it four months."

"In my work, I must be thorough."

"Please give it back to me," she said wearily. "Please let me go."

"We'll talk about that later," he said, and screwed the top back onto his fountain pen. Now, with the political charade over and done with, his manner became more relaxed, but also more serious. "Tell me what happened at Domingo's last night. A funny business, wasn't it?"

"No," she said, and shook her head slowly. "It wasn't funny."

"And that's why you can't sleep? Why your face is pale, and your eyes are like holes burned in a blanket?"

"I couldn't sleep, that's all I know."

"He tried to kill himself, eh? Was he drunk?"

"No, he wasn't. He looked sick and tired. But he wasn't drunk."

"I've heard various tales of what happened. From fishermen who invoked the Virgin so constantly in their recital that I was afraid she was involved. I want to hear your account now."

"He offered to shoot himself for a drink. Domingo must have thought he was joking. He gave him a drink, and then a gun. But he wasn't joking. He tried to kill himself. Domingo saved him."

"A joke, eh? And that's all you can tell me?"

Tani looked at him and nodded slowly.

Don Fernando said, "Do you know this American, Malcolm?"

"He came here one morning. He wanted something to drink. He made no sense at all. Jorge had to put him out."

Don Fernando paced the floor slowly. He stopped and looked with distaste at the collection of tiny plastic animals on the coffee table. Finally he said, "I trust you. I hope you realize that. I trust you to help me. Do you understand why?"

She turned her head aside, as if she were expecting a blow. "I understand," she said wearily.

"Precisely. I trust you because I know that you entered Spain illegally from Morocco, and that your behavior here has been an affront to the laws and morals of my country. If I gave this information to the Provincial Governor, he might put you in jail for five years. And it's worth remembering that our jails have not kept pace with the recent progress and prosperity in Spain. They are unpleasant places."

"Policemen," she said sighing, but her soft voice made the word vile.

"Naturally, you have a bad opinion of me," he said, as he began pacing again, restlessly and impatiently. "But even if I had no hold on you, I would trust you. I trust your brains, your discretion. It is strange, but I depend on you." He sat beside her and impulsively picked up her limp hand, but the touch of her flesh caused such a guilty warmth to spurt through him that he got quickly to his feet and began pacing again, shooting anxious glances at her from the corners of his eyes. "You imagine I am strong and secure," he said. "You think I take an unfair advantage of you, I know. Because you're a woman, and helpless, and all the rest of it. It's the fault of your sex to think that way. But it isn't true. I'm as

39

weak as you are. It's funny, isn't it? I walk the streets of the village, middle-aged, full of dignity, I, Don Fernando Gonzalez who has led a blameless life, and yet I feel that the buildings on either side might fall and crush the life out of me at any moment. What can be the reason for that?"

Tani shrugged and said nothing.

"Very well, let's talk of something more sensible," Don Fernando said irritably. "You know the American, Malcolm. Can you imagine where he is now? That poor drunken man? He sleeps in a comfortable room at the Pensione Royale with a terrace and a view of the sea. Clarke, the Englishman, sits with him like him like a nurse. Food and drink have been ordered for him, and Zarren, the Pole, is in the village this very moment trying to redeem his cameras and luggage. Does this make sense to you, Tani? Why should Domingo treat him like a brother?"

She said drily, "Perhaps he feels guilty at what he did to him."

"Yes, very likely. Domingo's last guilty thought probably occurred to him in his cradle." He looked at her frowning. "I want you to find out what it is between Domingo and the American. Never mind listening to college boys complain about our bad olive oil and rates of exchange. Forget all that nonsense for a while. If you are successful—" Don Fernando was so encouraged and stimulated by the hope that flared in her dark eyes, that he reached down and gently patted the back of her hand. "If you are, then there will be no difficulty about your passport."

"I can try, that's all," she said.

"Then you will succeed. For you can be a persuasive woman, Tani."

"But I can persuade you of nothing," she said bitterly.

"You dislike me, but you know only the worst side of me," he said. "That's the pity of my work. I can have no friends."

He bowed formally to her and left the room. Tani sat without moving for several moments, and then she sighed and slipped to the floor beside the coffee table and began to rearrange the positions of the brightly colored plastic animals. There was a childishly mutinous expression on her small face, as she moved a pink shepherd dog closer to the blue wolves which menaced her little herd of sheep.

6

THAT morning Domingo went to Malcolm's room in the Pensione Royale, which was near the beach. Clarke sat looking out at the sea, the stub of a cigarette plastered to his lower lip. His skin was gray and pallid in the strong morning light. He glanced around wearily when Domingo opened the door.

"He's still in the land of nod."

"Good." Domingo smiled with excitement as he pulled a chair over beside the bed. "I couldn't sleep all night thinking about him. Do you realize the possibilities?"

"I couldn't sleep listening to him sniffling and crying," Clarke said.

"Ah, the poor one." Domingo said with mock solicitude, and then he burst out laughing. "Of course he has nightmares. His brain must be on fire. We'll wet it down with brandy. You have plenty?"

"Enough for a forest fire!"

On the chest of drawers were several bottles of brandy, and a tray containing cold meats, cheese, bread, olives, and a pot of coffee.

"He ate nothing?" Domingo asked Clarke.

Clarke shook his head. "We pitched him onto the bed, and that was the end of him."

Malcolm still wore his soiled suit, his cracked shoes. Drops of sweat glistened on his face, and occasionally a tremor shook his body. He was breathing deeply and slowly. Domingo shook his shoulders. "Come on, wake up," he said.

Malcolm opened his eyes and looked at Domingo. For a moment he lay perfectly still, and then he grunted and twisted himself up to a sitting position on the bed. He seemed puzzled and confused as he stared blankly about the room. There was no expression on his face, but his matted hair and half-open mouth gave him the look of a sleepy idiot.

Domingo grinned and punched his shoulder. "You remember me?"

41

Malcolm frowned anxiously at him; he seemed to be making an almost physical effort to collect his thoughts. "Yes," he said in a thick, troubled voice. "Domingo?"

"He's smart this morning," Domingo said, and grinned at Clarke. "You remember me then. You know I'm Domingo. And do you remember this one with the skin like the belly of a snake?"

Malcolm looked at Clarke and nodded slowly.

"Good. You remember last night?"

"Yes, I remember."

"You tried to kill yourself. You tried to blow a hole through your head with my gun. You remember why?"

"We made a bargain. You gave me a glass of brandy. That's what it was worth to you."

"But you're sitting here, alive as I am. You didn't keep the bargain."

Malcolm wet his lips and shook his head helplessly.

Domingo snapped his fingers at Clarke without taking his eyes from Malcolm. "Bring me a bottle," he said, and when Clarke handed him the brandy Domingo held it out temptingly to Malcolm. He shook it gently so that the liquid flashed and sparkled in the sunlight. "I'm going to make another bargain with you," he said quietly; he was no longer smiling, and his eyes had become watchful. "You'd kill yourself for one drink? How much do you want to kill someone else?"

"You want me to kill somebody for you?" Malcolm said in a soft, wondering voice.

"Yes. Not today, not this week, maybe not this month. You do nothing until I give you the name of who I want you to kill. You sit in the room and stay drunk. I will give you all you need to drink." He poked Malcolm's chest with a finger the size of a banana. "It's a better bargain than last night, eh?"

"Yes," Malcolm said.

"You'll do it then? When I tell you to kill, you will do it?"

Malcolm nodded absently. "There's no reason not to."

"You'll really do it?" Domingo's face brightened with excitement. He took Malcolm's shoulders and shook him roughly and affectionately. "You'll do this for me? Kill anyone I tell you to?"

Malcolm rubbed a hand over his grimy face. "Yes, all right," he said.

The door opened and Zarren came in carrying two suitcases and a pair of cameras slung about his neck.

"Here are your clothes," Domingo said to Malcolm. "We

want you to be comfortable. Stay here and drink, be calm and happy." He bounced to his feet and gave Zarren a good-natured shove which sent him reeling across the room under the burden of luggage and cameras. "Unpack for him, put all his things away neatly," he said exuberantly. "You know how to take care of gentlemen, how to carry suitcases, bob your head like a monkey, put out the little paw for the tip."

Zarren dropped the suitcases on the floor, his whole body trembling with anger; even the tips of his blond mustaches seemed to be quivering with emotion.

"I was *concierge,* not waiter," he said as he knelt to un-buckle the straps about Malcolm's luggage.

Domingo smiled amiably; he was in a rare mood, almost drunk with happiness. "Forgive me, I was joking. I'm feeling good. I feel lucky." He dropped a hand on Malcolm's shoulder, in a gesture which suggested both respect and affection. "He will do it, Zarren. He agrees to do it."

"I don't like it," Zarren said stubbornly, as he began to put Malcolm's things away.

When he was through, the three men looked down at Malcolm, who sat on the edge of the bed, his eyes fixed stead-ily on the wall.

"You don't go out," Domingo said to him. "You stay here and drink." He tossed the bottle of brandy into Malcolm's lap. "The first payment on our new bargain. You understand?"

"I don't think he understands a bloody thing," Clarke said.

"He understands." Domingo twisted his hands into Mal-colm's coarse hair, forcing him to meet his eyes. "You un-derstand what I'm telling you?"

"I understood last night," Malcolm said slowly.

"Then you understand now," Domingo said.

He nodded to Clarke and Zarren, and the three men left the room.

Malcolm sat perfectly still, studying the reflections of sunlight on the brandy bottle in his lap. Then he picked up the bottle and stared at it. At last he put it aside, and got to his feet. Then he circled the room, inspecting it as warily as an animal in a new cage. There was a small terrace with a view of the sea, a bed, several chairs, a chest of drawers, and a bathroom with a stall shower, a handbasin, and a mirrored medicine cabinet.

On the chest of drawers was food. He began to eat, slowly at first, but then rapidly and hungrily.

The ham was fresh and pink, cut in transparently thin

43

slices, and he made sandwiches with the fresh bread and ate them with noisy relish. He drank the whole pot of warm coffee. The big olives he ate standing on the terrace and spitting the stones into the alley below him, while the fresh breeze off the sea cooled the sun on his face.

Malcolm didn't understand what had happened to him. And he made no attempt to analyze it. But he was curious to know what he looked like so he went into the bathroom, snapped on the light, and studied his face in the mirror over the handbasin. There was nothing in his reflection to indicate any change at all; all the bloodshot eyes and grimy features traced a portrait of unimportant filth on the shiny surface of the mirror. The changes must have been deep inside him, he decided; storms roaring in the void of his being, landslides and avalanches crashing tumultuously down the black abysses of his soul. He smiled tentatively then, for he realized that he was very close to understanding a very superior, very subtle joke.

He wondered what he would look like clean, but he knew instantly that was an absurd notion; the dirt didn't matter at all. But he pulled off his filthy clothes anyway and stood for half an hour under the shower, soaping and scrubbing himself ruthlessly. There were layers of grime on his body, it seemed; the water running off him was the color of mud. But he stayed in the shower until it flowed down his arms and legs as clear and bright as a crystal stream. Finally he shaved off his heavy growth of whiskers. He did the job without cutting himself once.

Then he studied himself once more in the mirror, his dark hair combed neatly into place, his skin smooth and clean from the razor, and he realized that it was true, that the grime, the dirt, the ugly externals concealed nothing of significance, nothing of value. And then he knew that he was very close to the heart of the joke.

There were clothes hanging in the closet that he hardly remembered; flannel slacks, cashmere sports jackets, loafers and brogues stretched smooth by wooden shoe trees. In the drawers were woollen socks, underwear, fashionably faded shirts from Brooks Brothers. He dressed with automatic care, selecting each garment and accessory with an almost forgotten taste and skill, discovering this dormant talent in the same way he had discovered the pleasures of food.

He put a chair on the terrace, but the morning glare was too harsh for comfort, so he rummaged about in his suitcases until he found a pair of sunglasses. He also found a large photograph of his dead wife and he placed this in a favorable light on the dresser and stepped back to study it for a moment.

He had taken the picture one autumn afternoon in a Paris cafe, and it was very good. It looked as if a breeze had touched her hair the exact instant the shutter was snapped. But he should have used a filter, he thought; in the blue-gray air the effect would have been haunting.

When he put on the sunglasses and sat on the terrace, the glaring sea was reduced to tones of amber and beige, and with a sigh of satisfaction Malcolm folded his arms and relaxed under the benign benediction of a lovely brown sun.

The news of what Malcolm had done the night before had spread through the village by noon. The pious folk prayed for his soul, but there were others who felt nagging doubts and odd cold pains in their bellies as they went about the crude, familiar work that day.

To the old priest Malcolm's act had been a blasphemous *nunc dimittis*, an exultant cry in praise of nothingness, and his feeble hands trembled at the affront to God as he raised the Host at the early morning Mass.

Several of the fishing boats did not put out to sea at dawn. Some of the men who had witnessed Malcolm's bargain with Domingo reflected on the uncertainty of the sea, the uncertainty of the day's catch, and the uncertainty of life itself. Their thoughts flitted uneasily about the notion that everything might be meaningless after all, and, as they examined this oddly seductive notion, they snuggled deeper in their blankets and ignored the entreaties of their wives and the cries and shouts of the owners of the fishing boats.

In the Bar Seville, which faced the coastal road running through Cartama to Gibraltar, three young Americans sat over coffee talking about Malcolm.

"He was drunk, that's all there was to it," Jeff Cooper said emphatically. He wore a flowing red beard, and his shoulders were wide and powerful, but there was something mild and uncertain about his eyes, as if he were accustomed to being confused by what he saw around him; and his high-crowned straw hat seemed more a device to hide his eyes from the world than to shade them from the brilliant sunlight, which now splashed luxuriantly against the whitewashed shops and homes of the village.

The young man sitting with him said, "Hell, there's no doubt of it. He's been so smashed for weeks that he couldn't hit the ground with his hat." He smiled appraisingly at the

45

girl who sat across the table. "I give him A for a good idea. But a big fat F for not doing it when he was sober." His name was Wayne Ludden III, and he came from Pennsylvania, and there was something so waspishly confident in his manner that everyone assumed that he was either very rich or very insecure. He wore a white T-shirt and faded army suntans, and his complexion was as soft as doeskin.

The girl laughed and said, "It bugs you guys, don't it?" She spoke in a mocking, spuriously tough voice. "Gets you right where you live, eh?" Her name was Dorothy Moore— Dorothea since she'd been in Spain—and she smiled with satisfaction as she saw the faint look of appeal in Jeff Cooper's mild eyes.

"Why should it bug me?" he said, shrugging.

"Dotty, dear, stop it," Wayne Ludden said. "When you rear back to get profound and bitchy I'd like to stick pins in you."

"The thing is, you envy Tony Malcolm."

"Envy him?" Jeff Cooper looked amused. "I feel sorry for the poor guy, that's all."

"Pure defensive reaction. He made the big gesture of denial you kids talk about making. And he got away with it. That's what you envy."

Dorothea Moore wondered irritably why she felt superior to them; she was no better and she knew it. Maybe that made the difference. They had deserted the take-charge generation in America to drink and strike poses in Spain, and they were stubbornly convinced that their defiance was significant and their rebellion genuine. They were more like sulking children being deliberately ignored by indulgent parents. Their defiance of American values, which they knew very little about, was only a petulant flutter, and they would return home as supplicants, hands out for jobs, but still believing that pennants of glory trailed in their wake.

And she was no better, of course. She had come to Spain a year ago to write a book. All that had happened to her was that she had got fat. It was a grotesque irony! She was a plump rebel, a stout figure of defiance, carved in bread and olive oil. That it had happened to her was maddening! She who longed so much to be a physical rebuke to all that was gross in the world; to stride through life tall and lean with dark, haunted eyes, hair streaming like a thunder-cloud from her brow. This had been her vision as she stalked the campus of a state teachers' college, and she hugged to her bosom the secret knowledge that she was not as others,

46

not like the creamy blondes and crew-cut idiots who were ripening like healthy vegetables before her eyes.

The book was inside her, a tangible, measurable proof of superiority. All she had needed was the year in Spain, and the patience to clothe the beauty inside her in shimmering words. But the words never came; she sat on the beach with her head full of them, but when she returned to her room to work, they had gone.

And no one had told her that Spain was cold in winter. Nothing had prepared her for the torture of numb hands and feet, of raw cheeks, and the stinging winds which lashed the rain against the windows of her room .Her only relief had been food; thick, tough cuts of meat covered with gravy, heavy stews made with fish and rice and potatoes, and the coarse bread layered with faintly ill-smelling butter. She couldn't help herself; it was her only comfort, and so her body had become thick and fat, and her skin so greasy that she made it a habit to wash herself and dab on lipstick without so much as glancing at her face in the mirror.

And now her money was gone, and her family's patience was at an end, and she would go home a failure. But she knew that, and she wasn't going to lie about it and claim this had been a year of growth and knowledge and mature rebellion.

That's what Jeff and Wayne wouldn't admit, and that's why they exasperated her so thoroughly. She stared at them now with a malicious smile creasing her plump cheeks.

"Don't you wish you'd done it?" she said slowly. "Shown the world your contempt as he did. Wouldn't that be a pleasant feeling to take back home with you?"

"Christ, write it all down, Dotty," Wayne Ludden said. "Put it in the big book."

Jeff Cooper stroked his long red beard thoughtfully. Then he said, "I don't feel that a gesture like that has any value unless it accomplishes something constructive." He realized sadly he was quoting what his father had once said to him; and he knew then that he would go home in the fall.

That afternoon Tani went to the Pensione Royale. There was a small lobby, and in the dim corridor leading toward the stairs an old woman was scrubbing the floor on her knees.

In Spanish, Tani asked her, "What room is the American in, please?"

"The crazy one? He is four floors up at the end of the hall."

Zarren was sitting slumped in a wicker chair in the lobby. Tani didn't see him until he stood and blocked her way as she turned toward the stairs.

"You can't see him," he said. He studied her face carefully, his nostrils flaring above the neat blond mustaches as if he were scenting for treachery and deceit in the air. "Why do you want to?" he said, noting the helpless, worried look on her face. "You could do nothing for him. He's filthy and drunk, probably unconscious by now."

"I want to talk to him."

"Why?"

"He stole something from me," she said quickly.

"What was it?"

She wet her lips. "A bracelet, yes, a bracelet. It wasn't worth much. Maybe he gave it away for something to drink. But I want to know where it is. Or I want the money for it."

"He has no money."

Tani looked about the lobby. "What is he using to stay here then?"

"Go home. Keep away from him. It's what Domingo wants. Do you understand?"

Tani sighed. "All right. But would you ask him to bring me my bracelet? Please?"

"He can't do that. Go home now."

Tani shrugged and left the Pensione Royale. Outside it was bright and warm in the sun. There was something lonely and vulnerable in the look of her small body as she wandered up the narrow street in the glaring sunlight.

7

THE maid who came to inquire about Malcolm's lunch was so confused by his appearance that she could only goggle at him in silence. She glanced nervously past him, as if looking for the filthy, unkempt scarecrow who had been carried into the *pensione* last night. At last she accepted the situation with a smile, and her cheeks became pink with pleasure as Malcolm looked courteously at the luncheon menu.

He decided on soup, and a steak, with fruit and cheese and coffee, and he asked the smiling girl if she would bring this to him in about an hour, for he had decided to take a walk before lunch.

She said she would do exactly as he wished, and then ran downstairs to the kitchen to tell her sisters and mother about him.

Malcolm slung the Leica about his neck, put on his sunglasses and went down to the lobby. Zarren rose and moved quickly between him and the door which opened on the street.

"What is this?" He seemed as puzzled as the maid had been by Malcolm's cleanly shaven face and casually good clothes. "You can't go out. You know that. Domingo wants you to stay in your room."

Malcolm looked across Zarren's bald head at the sunlight slanting in a single golden bar through the doorway, and observed how it seemed to chase the shadows into the corners of the small lobby. He frowned absently and set the timer of the Leica at one-fiftieth.

"I thought I'd take some pictures," he said.

"I don't like any of this," Zarren said. He seemed embarrassed by Malcolm's manner. "But I do what Domingo tells me to do. You cannot go out."

Malcolm looked at him with a thoughtful smile. "You have a gun?"

"Don't be a fool."

"I'm curious about what you're going to do. I suppose you'll knock me down. The women in the kitchen will scream for the police. What will you tell them? That you didn't want me to take pictures?"

Zarren looked uncomfortable; there were drops of perspiration on his forehead. "Be sensible. I told you I didn't like this business."

"Why do you do something you don't like?"

"There are things I need. To get them I do other things. It's that simple."

"I don't find that simple at all," Malcolm said. He sighed and took the lapels of Zarren's coat in his hands. "You're not to leave," he said, staring into his eyes. "Do you understand? You're my prisoner."

"Don't make me hurt you."

49

"What's the difference between you being my prisoner or my being yours? I'd like to understand that."

Zarren dipped a hand into his pocket and removed a clasp knife, the blade of which leaped out like the tongue of a snake at the pressure of his thumb. "Here's the difference," he said softly and put the tip of the blade against Malcolm's stomach. "Now go back to your room."

Malcolm laughed and leaned his weight against the point of the knife. "Go ahead, a twist of your hand will do it," he said. "Instead of taking pictures. I'll bleed to death." Malcolm removed his sunglasses and looked in Zarren's troubled eyes. "Just hold your wrist steady," he said quietly. "I'll do the job for you." But Zarren pulled the tip of the blade quickly from Malcolm's stomach and ran his tongue about his dry lips.

"You are crazy," he said, in a thick, helpless voice. "It's not worth killing you for."

"You are beginning to understand," Malcolm said.

He replaced his sunglasses and walked past Zarren, who turned slowly and stared after him with the haggard expression of a man who had just been unaccountably jarred by the weight of a shadow.

In the street Malcolm looked about critically; the light was clear and pure and there was an interesting pattern of shadows on the whitewashed buildings. In the shops were pink hams and golden brown partridges. Malcolm took a picture of a little boy reaching up to cool his hand in the burros' drinking fountain, and another of an old man in a black suit beating a goat.

He noticed a blonde young woman coming toward him with a shopping bag hanging listlessly in one hand. She wore shorts and a cone-shaped straw hat, and there was a look of irritation about her eyes and mouth, a suggestion of bone-deep discontent; it might have been caused by the flies buzzing around her bare limbs, a sick headache, or a general dissatisfaction with herself and the world at this particular moment, but its effect, Malcolm thought, offered an interesting contrast to the cheerful sunshine.

When she passed he took her picture from behind, trying to suggest the discontent in her face by the slump of her shoulders, the slow, dispirited swing of her bare legs.

He walked up the street and sat at a table on the terrace of the Bar Seville. The gray and purple hides of the mountains stretched up beyond the highway on which the traffic rumbled noisily toward Gibraltar or Málaga.

From the news kiosk an old man with rheumy eyes was crying out lottery numbers.

Malcolm looked at the mountains and thought about his dead wife. There was something ritualistic in this deliberate examination, for he realized that her face was fading in his memory, that her interest for him, dead or alive, was likewise fading, and that what he was doing now was saying good-bye to her, formally and politely, with a last token reminiscence.

All the cracks in him had been seared over, he knew; he was encased now in a protective shell that was as impervious to assault as the mountains before his eyes. In a crucible of shame and horror, weakness had been burned out of him, and it was thus that he had learned the ultimate truth, or the ultimate lie, about his existence. For inside this protective shell that had been forged so strongly and invincibly, there was nothing at all to protect; nothing to be guarded, nothing to be valued, nothing but emptiness. There was the essence of the joke, the preposterous, incredible truth of the joke.

Armies flanked with pennants flying to protect an empty castle! And when the slaughter was done, and the walls smashed, the invaders would provide a hearty laugh all around as they burst into the empty throne room.

He knew he was worthless, in the exact, literal sense of the word, and so it followed inevitably that his actions were without value, and that what was done to him, or was not done to him, could have no consequence. He didn't need to take the life of a stranger to prove this point to himself; but he owed Domingo for a brandy and so he would commit a gratuitous murder to settle that account. Then he would decide what to do, if anything, with the knowledge that had been burned into him. . . .

The terrace of the bar wasn't crowded at this hour. Tani sat alone sipping a glass of wine. The three young Americans who had been preparing to leave when Malcolm arrived, exchanged glances and ordered more coffee. Several elderly Spaniards played dominoes with deliberate care, and at another table were two young Germans in leather shorts and white shirts, decorated with bold red trim at the collar and cuffs. They were drinking bottles of imported beer in the sunlight. Their cheeks were flushed, their fine heads of blond hair shone like gold, and they exuded a sense of health and well-being that was as unmistakable as the sound of an exuberant yodel on a frosty morning.

But when they noticed Malcolm sitting alone at the far

end of the terrace, their manner became attentive and serious; after studying his quiet profile for a moment, the young Germans exchanged understanding glances and nodded slowly, as if they had reached a silent judgment on him.

Malcolm's motionless figure created a noticeable tension and embarrassment among the groups on the terrace. The Spaniards shifted their chairs discreetly to sit with their backs to him, the three Americans fixed their eyes on the top of the table with such intensity that their young faces suddenly looked furtive and conspiratorial.

Tani watched Malcolm covertly, hoping to catch his eye; she wanted to talk to him, but there was something in his steady, expressionless contemplation of the mountains which made her afraid to join him without invitation.

Malcolm was unaware of the tension he had created; he wasn't aware that there was anyone else on the terrace. He sat alone in perfect isolation, thinking idly of his dead wife.

Antonio, who owned the Bar Seville, came onto the terrace with an empty tray to collect glasses, but when he saw Malcolm he frowned and walked to his table.

"Is everything all right?" he asked him in a soft, worried voice.

"Yes, everything's fine."

Antonio smiled with an obvious effort, but his expression remained anxious. "Do you want—would you like a drink of anything?"

"No, thank you."

"Good," Antonio said with forced heartiness. Malcolm hadn't looked up at him, and Antonio shifted his weight awkwardly for a moment, trying to think of something to say, but finally he gave up and went off shaking his head in a manner that suggested both his concern and his confusion.

Malcolm found it difficult to concentrate on memories of his wife. He couldn't seem to keep her shadowy face clearly in focus, and he was no more successful when he thought of his parents, or various friends he had known over the years. In fact, everyone in his past seemed to have acquired a phantom quality; their forms and faces drifted palely and insubstantially through his thoughts, but when he tried to bring them into clearer view they became as blurred as figures in a fog.

He wasn't interested in them, in any case. It was an effort to remember them, to think of them, to recall the relationships and experiences which hinged them to his own life. Malcolm was interested only in himself, and so he dismissed

52

the phantoms and they retreated into the dark places in his mind.

He became aware of a slender child who had stopped to stare at him. She had bright blue eyes, direct and curious, and blonde hair streaked with sun. Her face was thin and quiet, and there was a scattering of freckles on her cheeks.

"You told me you liked to be dirty," she said with a note of accusation in her voice.

Malcolm removed his sunglasses. The little girl was frowning at him, her head cocked to one side on a stemlike neck.

"You said your nurse made you wash your hands all the time and change your clothes whenever you got dirty. So you stayed dirty when you grew up, because you liked to. It wasn't true, was it?"

"Why not?"

"You're all cleaned up now You shaved off your whiskers."

"The more things change," Malcolm said. "Do you know how the rest of that old saying goes?"

"No. Can I sit down?"

"Yes."

She seated herself with a curiously proprietary air and let her bare feet swing back and forth under the chair.

"I'll wait here for my mother," she said. "Can I have an orange drink?"

Malcolm looked through his pockets but he had no money. "No," he said.

"You know her, don't you? My mother, I mean. Her name is Coralee Davis."

"No, I don't."

"You looked so funny when I stopped to talk to you. Like you were almost asleep. What were you thinking about?"

"A dead woman."

"Did you know her? Did you like her?"

"She was my wife."

"Oh, that's too bad," the child said politely. After a deliberate pause, she looked at him shyly and said. "You don't remember me, do you?"

"I'm afraid not," Malcolm said.

"You asked me to get you some wine," she said, in a disappointed voice. "You told me it would be a joke on my mother. I thought you'd remember. I'm Jenny Davis, and our first names rhyme. Jenny and Tony." She sighed in a curious fashion, wistfully but impersonally, as if she might be contemplating a stranger's misfortune. "I told you about my father, too. Don't you remember that?"

"Get a drink from Antonio," Malcolm said. "You'll need it if you keep on talking."

"I thought you didn't have any money."

"I've got credit," Malcolm said. "For two bottles a day." She looked at him suspiciously. "You know something. I think you do remember me."

"Don't press your luck. Go get the drink!"

"I'll be right back." She slipped from her chair and ran into the bar. Across the street Malcolm saw Zarren standing beside the news kiosk, and staring at him with an expression of almost comical confusion. He looked as if he might continue this puzzled surveillance of Malcolm for all eternity; his stocky body and gleaming bald head bore the weight of the sun as patiently and impassively as a beast in a field.

Jenny's mother, Coralee, came along the narrow sidewalk in front of the Bar Seville just as her daughter rejoined Malcolm at his table. As she appraised Malcolm with a quick glance, Coralee moistened her lips, pushed a strand of hair from her forehead and greeted Jenny with a bright, indulgent smile.

"There you are, dear," she said, in tones which tripped along a half-octave above her normal speaking voice. "I couldn't imagine where you'd got to."

"I told you I wasn't going to the beach," Jenny said.

"It doesn't matter, dear," she said, including Malcolm in her warm smile.

As she seated herself beside Jenny, Malcolm realized that she was the same young woman whose expression of bone-deep discontent he had tried to catch on film just a short while ago.

They exchanged names, and Coralee confessed to him that she would hardly know anyone in Cartama if it weren't for her daughter. "Jenny makes friends with everyone, and then kindly introduces them to her somewhat proper mother," she said, but with a complacent smile which suggested that her propriety, far from being oppressive or stuffy, was merely a defense against unrewarding contacts. "Actually, I avoid the tourist crowd," she went on, lowering her voice discreetly. "It's not snobbishness, for heaven's sake, but I simply feel you learn so much more from the natives in a foreign country. I mean about their attitude toward life and politics, things like that. I don't speak Spanish too well, but I understand everything they say.

54

You'd be surprised at the information I've even been able to glean from our maid, Anna."

Jenny looked at her mother with a smile. "All Anna talks to me about is her wedding dress and her brother's children," she said.

"She's more serious with me, of course," Coralee said. She regarded her daughter with narrowed eyes, searching that small face for secret evidence of mockery or insolence. "Naturally Anna wouldn't talk to you about politics."

"She doesn't know where Madrid is," Jenny said, and her small jaw hardened as she stared at her mother. "She doesn't know where Gibraltar is, either. I'm going to ask her what she talks to you about."

Coralee smiled helplessly at Malcolm. "You can't be interested in our maid's political viewpoints, in any case. What I'm wondering is, would you like to come to a small party I'm giving next week? It will be a grab-bag crowd, but you might find it amusing. Where are you staying?"

"At the Pensione Royale."

"I'll leave a note there with the time and date. Have you been in town long, Mr. Malcolm?"

"It seems as if I have," Malcolm said.

"I know what you mean," she said with a quick, comradely smile. "I have that feeling, too. We must really run now. Come along, dear."

"Thanks for the drink," Jenny said.

"Oh, dear, my little beggar's been up to her usual tricks, I gather."

"Not at all," Malcolm said. "I owed her a drink, you see."

"Oh, I'm sure you did," Coralee said and smiled indulgently at him. "Now come along, Jenny."

They waved a good-bye to him and started down the street, but after they had gone about twenty yards, Jenny stopped abruptly, said something to her mother, and ran back to Malcolm.

"Do you like her?" she asked him in a quick little voice. "My mother, I mean."

"I know one thing," Malcolm said. "You don't."

She sighed helplessly. "It's not that. I *do* like her. But I hate it when she makes me feel sorry for her."

"Jenny, I don't think it matters."

"Well, if that's true, it's very nice," she said comfortably. "I'll come and visit you. I'll bring the party invitation, you watch."

She grinned and ran off down the street to join her mother.

The two young Germans had been watching Malcolm, and now they exchanged glances, stood with almost military precision, and walked across the terrace to his table.

They were strikingly tall and handsome, strong and golden in the sunlight, but their eyes struck an odd note in this symphony of splendid physical vigor; they were intelligent and penetrating, luminous with sympathy and compassion.

"Please," one of the Germans said by way of apology and placed a small white business card on the table. "It is not our intention to disturb you now."

They smiled at him pleasantly, inclined their heads in a formal bow, and then they returned to their own table to finish their beer.

Malcolm looked at the card. Engraved on one side were two names: Karl Webber and Willie Maganer. In ink below them was the name of a hotel in Torremolinos, the Pez Espada. He turned the card over. On the back was a message written in a small precise hand. The message read: "Perhaps we can explain what you really meant to do last night. Please call us. It would be of mutual interest."

There was no signature.

Malcolm was aware that the two Germans were watching him. He turned the card over several times in his hand, and finally tucked it away in the inside pocket of his jacket. The Germans acknowledged his gesture with approving smiles. One raised his glass to Malcolm in a discreet salute; the other continued to smile steadily at him, as if this mysterious series of gestures and responses had somehow united them all in an amusing conspiracy.

8

AT Domingo's that afternoon they were playing cards. and Domingo's mood was fine for he had been winning consistently from Paco and Clarke and Zarren.

The bar was quiet and the glasses and bottles sparkled cleanly in the sunlight. The window facing Domingo framed a rectangle of blue sea and white sky like a painting, and it seemed to him that the scene belonged exclusively to him, that it existed only for his pleasure, that this rigidly delineated beauty was literally unavailable to anyone else in the world; for to enjoy it, a person would have to seat himself in Domingo's own chair, and such a transgression was beyond the realm of possibility.

Clarke said, "Since you still trust him, why don't I leave for Gibraltar tomorrow?"

"There's no hurry," Domingo said, smiling as he studied the cards which looked no bigger than postage stamps in his great hands.

"And why do you trust him?" Zarren demanded bitterly. "I told you he left his room. You insist it doesn't matter. He sits in the cafe, talks with people, drinks nothing. He is clean, he has put on good clothes, and you say none of that matters."

"What matters is the first thing you told me about him," Domingo said gently. "That he offered to let you put a knife in him for no reason at all. I know now he will pay me for that glass of brandy. The rest isn't important. It is better if he is seen in the village. He looks like anyone else, enjoying the sun and good weather." Domingo smiled voluptuously, as if the deepest springs of pleasure in his body were trembling under the caress of exhilarating winds. "But he is nothing but a bullet," he said in a soft, dreaming voice. "I can point him in any direction I want. I can fire him as I would fire a gun."

Clarke stared at Domingo's flushed, excited face, and concealed his disgust with an effort which almost nauseated him. "Then let's get on with it, for God's sake," he said. "Let's use him."

"No, we will wait," Domingo said, smiling appreciatively at the three queens he found in his hand.

"You enjoy knowing what you can make him do," Zarren said quietly. "You like that feeling. Isn't that the truth?"

Domingo glanced at him guiltily, like a child caught in a shameful act. But there was a grudging respect in his expression. "I think of you as a quiet, patient ox," he said. "I'm wrong, eh? You understand more than you show." Domingo put down his cards and frowned thoughtfully. "Yes, it's a pleasant feeling, I admit it. I have never feared anyone physically. The ones I feared were always far above me, beyond my reach, and from that distance they had the power to hurt or destroy me." He glanced slowly around the table, scanning each face deliberately with his tiny eyes. "Do you

57

realize I could kill practically anyone now? The most important man in the world has the muzzle of a gun against his head, and my hand is on the trigger. It seems almost a pity to waste our bullet on a lesser target." Then his mood changed, and he laughed and pushed chips into the middle of the table. "Think of that, while I win your money."

Clarke felt anger gnawing at his breast like a small, ferocious animal. He didn't trust himself to look at Domingo, who was smiling so broadly that his piggish little eyes had almost disappeared in the hard rolls of fat above his cheeks. Instead, Clarke ran a hand despairingly over his gray face, and thought, "Sweet Christ, he'll ruin everything for all of us." He had fought every minute and day of his life, it seemed to Clarke, and now that he couldn't fight any more it was his putrid luck to be dependent on this fat, bullying Frenchman. He had fought on the docks of Liverpool for bread, and he had fought in Germany and after that in Asia and Algeria, for money instead of the Queen. It wasn't that he liked it, it was his trade, something he'd gotten into by accident, as he might have become a carpenter or shoemaker, and he didn't know any other way to keep himself in gin and cigarettes. But one day his nerve had gone. It hadn't been dramatic, like in a film, cowering under a barrage or going soft as butter at the sight of a chum being blown to bits. No, he'd been sipping tea in a comfortable hotel in Algiers, on leave from his company, when suddenly his hands began to shake without warning. He went up to his room and lay on the bed, trembling as if he had a fever, and that was the end of fighting for him.

This job with Domingo was worth six hundred pounds, enough to rent a room and keep him alive while he looked around for a job. He wanted to be alone as much as possible the rest of his life, in a quiet room with a strong lock on the door where he could think about the things that made him happy—or less miserable, anyway—with gin and cigarettes at hand, and the air so warm that he would lie without any clothes on and know that he was safe and alone and through forever with the rest of the whole flipping world.

That was Clarke's dream, and Domingo was threatening to turn it into a nightmare.

Zarren said, "We wait then." He looked steadily at Domingo. "But for how long? I need the money."

"We wait until I decide we are ready."

"I am in no hurry," Paco said, smiling at Domingo, eager

to please him, and he was rewarded with a friendly clap on the shoulder, and a quick, suggestive wink.

"You're happy to wait, eh?" Domingo said. "You have things to keep you busy?"

"There is much available."

"The American? How is she? Does she make you help with the dishes, do the shopping? I read that's how they are."

"She cries when I leave her," Paco said, grinning modestly. "I tell her I can't see her, and she becomes desperate. She wants me only to herself, because she feels that would be more like a marriage."

Domingo laughed and tossed a hundred peseta chip into the pot. "Zarren, you and Clarke must find something like Paco to keep you busy. You should have luck, for you don't have it at cards. I have all the luck. Lady Luck smiles on me. All the ladies of luck are smiling on me," he said, grinning with delight at this oblique allusion to the three queens he was holding in his hand.

In the days that followed the sun was warm and brilliant, but the cold winds at dawn, and the shaggy, thickening coats of the burros, warned the fishermen and farmers that the wheel of the seasons was turning inexorably toward the stinging bitterness of winter. The tourists were beginning to leave; winter geraniums glowed in the keen dry air, the last of the little green melons ripened in the markets, and there were sparkles of dew on the grass in the early morning.

Malcolm occupied himself in those days by photographing the streets and shops of Cartama, and the mountains above the village. To some extent, he was losing his mantle of notoriety; his behavior was so conventional that no one paid much attention to him any more. Also the story of what had happened at Domingo's had become so garbled in the retelling that now even the eye-witnesses were confused and vague about the details.

Malcolm was conscious of his new isolation, but not at all disturbed by it. The tempo of his existence seemed to have been reduced to a slow and languarous beat; as he drifted along the streets of the village or the trails in the hills, he felt as if he were moving effortlessly through a shimmering dream. It was as if a great golden bell had been placed over the whole village, and within this shining vacuum every sound and movement had been attenuated beyond the range of the human sensory apparatus; it was as if everyone had entered a conspiracy of silence, and Malcolm found it easy to imagine that all the persons around him were tiptoeing through life with fingers pressed warningly to their lips.

In this unnatural but not unpleasant lacuna, Malcolm let his cameras trap the reality of his surroundings; he abandoned his usual techniques and tricks, and tried to catch the look of things as simply as possible. As a commercial photographer, he had trained his eye to find irony and humor in human situations. Better than that, of course, was "story": the Ambassador's wife sleeping through her husband's speech, the frightened African child weeping at the strange discomfort of his first pair of shoes.

Now he was trying to be more honest. There was no truth in photographing the village from the mountains so that it looked only like a cluster of white and lovely shells strewn along the beach. Nor was there truth in using the lens like the snout of a pig to root up only dirt and filth and the stench of chamber pots. There must be balance.

One cool, sunny afternoon he stopped on the rocky trail above the Arroyo de Miel, and stared down at the sea. He studied the water and the beach in an attempt to find a relationship between the fishing nets strung out to dry on the sand and the waves that broke like angrily tumbled lace along the shore line. The physical world had its share in creating mankind's moods, of course; shadows, colors, lines, objects dense and massive, others translucent and nebulous, all spread carelessly and haphazardly about to make their billion whimsical impressions on every human eye and ear and nerve.

He thought carefully and tenaciously about such matters; he didn't think of the time when he would have to pay his debt to Domingo.

As he took the shot of the beach and lowered his camera, he saw that someone had come up the trail, and had stopped to watch him. She wore blue jeans and a white shirt, and Malcolm had the odd notion that he had seen her before, although he couldn't imagine where. She was young and slim, with thick black hair knotted behind her head, and her eyes were dark and luminous in her small brown face. Eurasian, he thought, noting her skin, her almond-shaped eyes, and the gravity of her manner.

"I saw you pass my house," she said. "Can I talk to you?"

"You live in the Arroyo de Miel?" he asked her.

She nodded slowly, appraising him with dark, glistening eyes. "We could go to my house and talk. There's coffee, things to drink." She came closer to him, moving with a suggestion of sinuous languor, in spite of her flat sandals and boyish clothes. "You through taking pictures?" she said, smiling at his camera. She had very white teeth.

"What do you want to talk to me about?"

She seemed to deliberate, watching him with her dark eyes. Then she said simply, "I need some help."

"From me?"

"Yes."

"You better try somebody else," Malcolm said. "Why not ask God? He bucked for the job. Of course, *His* story was that he didn't care about the stripes, it was just the money he wanted. But nobody believed that for a minute."

"What's the matter with you?" She was still smiling at him, her head tilted slightly to one side, but there was a look of confusion about her eyes. "You drunk or something?"

"No, I'm not drunk."

"You can help me. Please."

"I doubt it, Tani."

Yes, that was her name, he realized; but how had he known that?

"Have I met you before?"

"Yes, you came to my house early one morning. You were drunk." She studied his face and eyes carefully then, searching them for memory or recognition, but as he continued to regard her pleasantly but neutrally, she went on with more confidence, the words tumbling from her lips with a certain childish charm. "Oh, yes, you were very drunk, and all you wanted was something to drink, nothing else, so I gave you some brandy, and you rested and smoked a cigarette and felt very much better, of course."

"You were good to me? Patient, generous, kind?"

She dismissed his words with a smile. "What is a little brandy? A cigarette?"

"How can I help you?"

"What is happening with you and Domingo?"

"Nothing at the moment. Why should that interest you?"

"It's not for me. It's for someone else."

"All right," Malcolm said. "He wants me to kill someone for him."

She put a hand to her mouth, and shook her head quickly. "It isn't good to joke like that."

"You have the story of my relationship with Domingo," he said. "I hope you can sell it or trade it for something profitable."

She stared at him in silence, her eyes moving fearfully over his features. "You are going to do it? Kill someone?"

"Yes."

"Who is it?"

"I don't know." Malcolm held his light meter close to her small, frightened face, then adjusted his F-stop and smiled at her. "Come on, say *'fromage.'* I'm going to take your picture."

"Cheese," she said weakly.

Malcolm snapped the shutter, and knew that he had caught it all, the cold wind tugging at her hair, the pinched look of her face, the alarm flashing in her eyes. Then he said, "Have I earned a cup of coffee?"

Tani crossed her arms and hugged herself tightly, as if her slim body had suddenly been exposed to a bitter wind. The gesture was childish and revealing, Malcolm thought; it was the reaction of a totally vulnerable human being, and he was puzzled by it. What could she possibly have to lose in life, except perhaps some long-cherished pain?

"You asked me about Domingo and I told you," he said.

"I'm afraid," she said helplessly. "I don't want to know."

"Very well, we won't talk about it any more." He slung the Leica about his neck, and took Tani's arm in a firm grip. "We'll talk about you instead."

She gave him a wary, puzzled glance, trying to guess at his intentions or needs. But she learned nothing from his eyes or his face. She suddenly felt weak and helpless. She disliked the pressure of his hand on her arm, but she was afraid to pull away from him. Feeling frustrated and apprehensive, she allowed him to guide her down the curving trail to her home in the Arroyo de Miel.

Tani was used to telling men her life story. It was a part of the game. They liked talking about it afterward, she knew, about how they were friendly with a prostitute, and had learned from her own lips how she had got into the business, and what some men had done to her and so forth. Tani had a dozen stories to choose from, not from any wish to disguise or embellish her background, but simply to save boring herself to distraction; she could amuse herself, to some extent, by pretending to be a Bomb Victim, a Madame Butterfly, a Gutter Child, or the bastard daughter of the Emperor himself—anything at all was possible in these autobiographical fancies. But for some reason she told Malcolm the truth. Perhaps because she had an uneasy feeling that he would know if she lied to him. She told him of her life in Paris before her mother died, and of the man who provided for her then on the explicit condition that she would provide for him when she was old enough to. It made her sad and wistful to talk about her funny little mother to a stranger, and to remember the hazy blue days beside the river. Malcolm hadn't asked for this information, and from his expression she couldn't tell whether he was interested in it or not; he sat looking at the sea while the afternoon faded away, and long shadows fell against the rosy sides of the mountains. There was no expression at all in his face.

Finally she was silent.

"It was good coffee," he said then.

"Do you want some more?"

He shook his head slowly and picked up one of the brightly colored little animals which grazed on the slick surface of the coffee table. For what seemed a long time to Tani, he stared at it in silence.

"I like to play with them," she said, made uneasy and defensive by his frowning examination of the little plastic animal.

She sat on the floor beside the table. "Look, I can frighten the sheep with the wolf, and then I send the big brave shepherd dog to protect them."

"It's a game with a happy ending," he said.

"Why are you doing what Domingo wants you to?" she asked him anxiously.

"Because I must," Malcolm said.

"That's foolish. Is it because of the night in his bar? When you tried to kill yourself for a drink?"

"That's part of it."

"You are a fool," she said, and for the first time she had no fear of him; there was anger and indignation in her voice. "Listen to me: it was a drunken thing you tried to do. You were sick, helpless. I lied to you. I wasn't kind to you when you came here that morning. I laughed at your sorrows, Jorge kicked you into the street."

He smiled at her. "Yes, I know that."

"I thought you didn't remember," she said hesitantly.

"I remembered."

"But don't you see, you were drunk. You mustn't let Domingo make you kill someone."

"What I do for him, I will do out of gratitude," Malcolm said.

He laughed at her puzzled frown and felt a mild pity for this uneasy, troubled child. Tani smiled at him then, but hers was the polite, professional smile of a courtesan, and it suggested that while he held her interest totally, she wouldn't presume to evaluate the products of his superior mind.

"Do you understand me?" he asked her.

"I would like to be free, too," she said sadly.

"How can I help you?"

Tani put aside her fears with an effort of will; she ignored the premonitions of disaster that had made her heart flutter so nervously. She leaned closer to him, and her smile became eager and childishly pleasing. "Tell me all you know about Domingo. Who he wants you to kill. What he will gain from it."

"And who will you sell or trade this information to?"

Tani considered her reply carefully. Finally she decided there was no advantage in lying. "To Don Fernando, the policeman."

"And he will pay you well?"

"He will set me free. He will give me my passport. I cannot leave without it. I want to go to Paris, but now it is like I am chained to the wall in a dungeon." She smiled piteously at him, and crossed her wrists and bowed her head in a timeless posture of helplessness.

"What right has he to keep your passport?"

"I came here from Morocco on a boat that landed whiskey near Marbella. I have no visa. In Madrid I know the name of a man who can forge one for me."

"Why not buy a fake passport? I've heard that can be arranged."

"You don't understand," she said with a helpless sigh. "If I leave the village, Don Fernando will notify Madrid that he has my true passport, and if I try to leave Spain I must be carrying a fake one. They can put me in jail then, he tells me, and the jails here are very bad."

"Why does he hate you so much? Or is it the other way around?"

"I don't know. Something is wrong with him. He has no confidence. I think he feels I am lucky for him."

Malcolm smiled, for it seemed to him the situation was incredible enough to be comical; in the short time since he had taken leave of the world, he had nearly forgot its pointless agonies and fears. That people still cried out in terror at meaningless threats struck him as both ridiculous and remarkable. But mingled with his astonishment was a certain compassion, for obviously this poor simple girl had no way of knowing the truth of things; she hadn't been exposed to the ultimate joke as yet.

"All right, I'll help you," he said.

"Then I will make you happy," Tani said eagerly.

"Good God, spare me that."

"I only mean I will be good to you, so good your face will never be sad again. I will do anything you want."

"I want nothing," he said.

Tani laughed softly and confidently then, calm and sure of herself for the first time that afternoon. She was pleased and excited by a challenge to her professional skills. Kneeling beside his chair she smiled and put her cheek against his knee. "Maybe you will want something," she said. "I think you will, I bet." She laughed again, her white teeth flashing in the soft late sunlight, and then she slipped her hand through the buttons of his shirt and drew her fingertips sharply across his bare stomach.

9

AFTER lunch Malcolm stretched out on the bed in his room. Soon afterward there was a knock on the door. He lay still, hoping whoever it was would go away, for he had become fond of his silent empty life, and the time he found available to explore and assess his own background and experiences. In some mysterious fashion his unconscious seemed to have become accessible to him; he had the illusion that he could physically lower himself through layer after layer of murk and gloom, until at last he came to locked vaults and storerooms in the ultimate depths of his being, where all the black twisted memories of his life were locked away in the darkness. It was an incredible and wonderful sensation, completely without fear or anxiety, for now there were brilliant lights to see by, and all the doors stood open, and Malcolm could stroll slowly from one subterranean chamber to the next, examining the dark, averted face of the past with clinical, good-humored interest.

But the knock was repeated, and Malcolm got up and opened the door. Jenny Davis stood in the corridor.

"I came to invite you to my mother's party," she said, in her soft, excited voice. "It's for tomorrow night, after dinner. About nine. Can I come in?"

She sat on the straight-backed chair and looked about with frank curiosity, her blue eyes lively and bright against her tanned skin. "You've got a nice terrace," she said, nodding toward the sea. She wore a pink dress with tiny white flowers stitched about the collar, and her hands and face were very clean. "I wanted to see where you lived," she said smiling. "Do you like Cartama?"

"Yes, I think so."

"We didn't at first. Mommy hated it. But now she's changed her mind. We may stay all winter."

"Would you like that?"

"When Mommy's happy it's all right anywhere."

"And she's happy now?"

"Well, I think she is." She frowned faintly, as if uncertain of how to explain this phenomenon. "It's because of Paco, I guess. She likes him."

Malcolm had noticed Paco and Coralee together in his tours of the village. They strolled the streets, chattered over coffee in the cafes, went hand in hand up the trails to the mountains. Coralee rode behind him on his bright little scooter, laughing inordinately at this madness, and hugging Paco's slim waist with happy, possessive excitement.

"So your mother and Paco are good friends?"

"Yes, he comes by every day. And he has dinner with her at night. They must like each other a lot. Eating with someone you don't like must be terrible. I guess they'll get married."

"Would you like that?"

She sighed gently. "I don't know. But he's going to be rich. That would be nice. I could go to school in Switzerland. We've already got the catalogues. The girls ride and play tennis and walk across into France for chocolate when the weather is nice. But that's a special treat. It's only four times a year."

Something rang a bell in Malcolm's mind; and that illusion of sound reminded him of Tani's name. "So Paco's going to be rich, eh?" He smiled at Jenny. "How will he manage that little trick?"

"I don't know, but he brags a lot to Mommy. He doesn't tell me anything much. I asked him once, because he was

66

talking about buying a boat to sail in, and he said boom-boom, and started laughing as if that was the funniest joke in the world."

"Boom-boom?"

"That's what he said. Mommy laughed too, so I guess it must be funny." She stood abruptly. "I've got to go now. Can you come to the party."

Boom-boom! That meant guns then, Malcolm thought. If he could find out a bit more, it shouldn't be too difficult to piece together a story that Tani could trade to the policeman for her passport.

"Will Paco be there?"

"Oh, sure."

Malcolm decided to go to the party. "Tell your mother I'll be happy to come."

Jenny hesitated at the door. She looked up at him uncertainly. "Would you do me a favor?"

"Yes, if I can."

"You can, but only if you want to. Would you kiss me good-bye? Would you, please?"

"We can only be good friends, you understand," Malcolm said, trying to tease a smile from her grave little face. "Because I've got a gal in Kalamazoo, and she'd hit the ceiling if she thought I was traipsing around with some little blonde in Spain."

Jenny turned swiftly for the door, averting her face from him, but he had already seen the helpless flash of tears in her eyes. He took her shoulders, and turned her around gently. "Now what's the matter?" he said, and sat on the edge of the bed so that he could look directly at her unhappy face. "Come on, what is it?"

"I just don't want you to laugh at me, that's all," she said, the words spaced by the catch in her voice.

"I'm sorry, Jenny." He pulled her close and kissed her damp smooth cheek. "Are we friends again?"

"I guess so."

"All right, as a friend, can I ask you this: do you miss your father very much?"

She turned her head to one side and looked down at the floor. "Yes, I miss him," she said.

"How often do you see him?"

"I don't see him at all. I never will see him," she said. "It's what Mommy calls a package deal. He didn't want either of us any more."

"You can't visit him?"

"No, he's got two other children now. I mean, the woman he married had them already. They don't want us to get mixed up together. I really do miss him and it hurts all the time." She began to cry then, and Malcolm pulled her close to him and held her tightly in his arms.

Finally her sobs diminished and she straightened and said, "I've got to go. I'm sorry I started crying."

Malcolm took his handkerchief and dabbed at the tears on her cheeks. "Let me tell you something," he said. "If you're crying for him, that's fine because he's a fool. But if you're crying for yourself, stop it. In the first place it won't help things one damn bit. Secondly, your lonely little pain will dry up and wither away if you stop nourishing it with tears. Thirdly, Jenny dear, nothing matters one way or the other, so why not live with the truth, instead of agonizing over a lie?"

She had stopped crying and was watching him with doubtful eyes. "You're sure? You're sure it doesn't matter?"

"Yes, I'm sure."

"You told me that before," she said, in a thoughtful little voice. "But that's not what other people think. So how do you know you're right?"

"All right, I can't prove it," he said. "But you've been looking at the world the way the world told you to look at it. The way the world likes to be looked at. As if it were big and important and made sense. And all you've got out of it is a broken heart. Try my way and see what happens."

She tilted her head to one side and looked thoughtfully at him. "Well, I just might," she said, and her manner was so judicious and practical that Malcolm almost burst out laughing.

Later he marvelled at the heartaches she had endured and the blind, vicious cruelties which had been practiced on her by her parents. He lay on his bed staring out at the sea, and his thoughts drifted to Tani. Tomorrow night he must try to learn something about a gun or guns from Paco. He hadn't seen Tani since that first afternoon a week ago, and he had difficulty remembering her with any clarity, but he did remember his promise to help her. All these people, and all their problems, were phantoms to him, as unreal as the faces and voices in his past.

To Malcolm now there was only one reality; the voyage to the past, riding the trades which bore him swiftly inward to the dark waters of his own guilts and fears and needs.

With a smile of anticipation, he closed his eyes and let his thoughts drift with the ugly currents. . .

The party that Jenny's mother gave followed an informal, inexpensive pattern; the garden and maids of the *pensione* she was staying at were borrowed for the night, bowls of punch were set out on tables, and music was added by an ancient, hand-cranked victrola. There were eighteen or twenty guests, and about half of them stood about the punch bowls while the others danced on the brick floor of the garden. It was a lovely night, with a half-moon that looked close enough to touch, and cool breezes stirring the bougainvillea which grew lushly along the garden walls.

Almost everyone dressed casually, the women in slacks and sweaters, the men in jackets without ties. Malcolm was one exception to the sartorial informality; he wore a dark suit, a wool knit tie, and a white shirt with silver cuff links which Janey had given him on their first wedding anniversary. Another exception was provided by a tall, middle-aged Englishman with a cold face and disapproving mouth, who had arrived promptly at the stroke of nine o'clock wearing a conservative gray suit, a vest brightened discreetly by a narrow gold watch chain, and a regimental tie.

He spoke briefly with Malcolm. His name was Gregory Neville. He was in Spain on a short holiday. This was his third day in Cartama and a certain twitch of his thick brown mustaches made it clear he considered that about three days too long. Gregory Neville wrote detective novels. He was obviously bored with the party and bored with Malcolm, and, at a pause in their conversation, he smiled distantly at him, murmured an excuse and strolled off to the other side of the garden.

Malcolm sat against the wall on a stone bench and looked at the dancers and listened to the gay, splintered music pouring from the throat of the old victrola. There were halves of oranges bobbing drunkenly about in the punch bowls, and the cigarette smoke was whipped around like thin gray scarves in the brisk wind. He noticed Clarke, who stood alone staring at Paco and Coralee Davis with an expression of mild disgust on his small gray face. They were dancing near him, so slowly and suggestively that it seemed obvious they were lost to everything in the world but themselves.

Suddenly Malcolm blinked his eyes, and his heart began to pound like a hammer against his ribs. In the soft moonlight, a curious transformation seemed to be taking place among the men and women in the garden.

They were slowly turning into skeletons.

Malcolm knew this must be an illusion, some disorderly projection of his mind or his optical nerves. He blinked his eyes rapidly, and pressed his fingers against his temples, but the strange illusion persisted stubbornly, and Malcolm felt his flesh crawling as he stared in helpless fascination at the grinning skulls, the ugly, saucer-shaped pelvic depressions, the spindly, ash-white assortment of rib cages and thigh bones which were gyrating before him in the silvery moonlight.

He had no notion how long this grotesque hallucination lasted, but it was shattered at last by a friendly voice and the pressure of a hand on his shoulder.

"You don't look very happy."

Paco sat down beside him and patted his shoulder gently. "Maybe you need a drink, eh?"

"No, I'm all right," Malcolm said, shaking his head slowly. The illusion had vanished, and now a garden-full of properly fleshed and properly clothed men and women laughed and chatted and danced before his eyes.

"You don't want a drink, that's very strange, very funny," Paco said. He was cheerfully tight himself, his eyes sparkling merrily, and a flush of excitement darkening his slim handsome face. "I am very happy," he said to Malcolm. "I am very lucky."

His contentment with himself was inoffensive, Malcolm thought; there was no challenge or intelligence in his smoothly ordered features, only a healthy, animal satisfaction that was no more significant than the purring of a well-fed cat or the aimless exuberance of a pony.

At the entrance to the garden Malcolm saw Coralee Davis greeting the tall young Germans who had left their card on his table at the Bar Seville. Malcolm had forgot about these splendidly handsome and healthy young men, and the strange message which had been written on the back of their calling card.

The taller of the two young Germans towered a foot above Coralee, his elegantly sculptured blond head gleaming in the candlelight which flickered from lanterns hanging in the trees. They both wore dark suits with white silk ties, and glittered tastefully with rings and cuff links and wrist watches.

Coralee noticed Malcolm sitting with Paco, and waved gaily

to him. The two Germans followed the gesture with their eyes, and when they saw Malcolm their faces lit up with pleasant smiles of recognition, and they bowed to him with easy formality.

He expected them to come over and talk to him, but instead they turned away with Coralee and joined a group standing about one of the punch bowls.

Coralee looked radiant. Happiness, excitement, self-confidence—whatever she was getting from Paco—had smoothed the lines of discontent from her face, leaving it smooth, bland and cheerful, but as empty of meaning as a doll's smile. She wore a red shawl about her bare shoulders, stiff with beads and busy with tassels, and her piled-up blonde hair was clamped in place with a rhinestone barrette. In one hand she carried a rose. It would be between her teeth before the night was over, Malcolm thought.

"You're a lucky man," he said to Paco.

"I'm happy, it's the same thing," Paco said.

"You've got everything. You're young, healthy, handsome, and everybody likes you."

Paco smiled and without excessive modesty said, "I have everything, yes. But I deserve it, I believe. I have worked for it. Some people are unhappy and do nothing about it. But I know how the world is."

"And you're going to have lots of money, too," Malcolm said. He smiled steadily at Paco. "Boom-boom, eh?"

Paco's own smile suddenly went awry; his lips tightened across his strong white teeth, and a tiny tic began to pull rhythmically at the corner of his mouth. He looked uneasily at Malcolm. "What does that mean?"

Malcolm continued to smile, as he watched Paco's nervously shifting eyes. "Guns, *amigo*, what else? Boom-boom!"

Paco fidgeted anxiously; he rubbed his forehead, glanced quickly about the garden, tried unsuccessfully to smile, and then sighed and leaned closer to Malcolm.

"I didn't know they told you," he said, barely whispering the words.

"Oh, I'm in on everything," Malcolm said confidently. "I'm the guy who rigs the tilt sign on their pinball machines."

Paco frowned at him, for they were speaking English, and he hadn't understood Malcolm's last comment. *"No comprendo,"* he said helplessly.

"It's not important. Only the guns are important."

"Who told you about them? Domingo?"

Malcolm winked solemnly at him. *"Claro!"*

"It's not good to talk about it," Paco said, running a finger under the collar of his shirt. "If he told you it's all right, but still it's better to say nothing."

Coralee swept over to them and put an end to their conversation. She dropped a hand on Paco's shoulder and her fingernails stood out like neat, pink-tipped claws against the white fabric of his jacket. There was a group setting out for Torremolinos later, she told Malcolm, to dance and bob for olives, and would he care to join them? Malcolm declined regretfully.

Coralee put the stem of the rose between her teeth and began to snap her fingers in a fair approximation of a flamenco beat. "You don't know what you're missing," she said, and throwing back her head, she laughed until tendons stood out slimly against the crepy skin of her throat.

Malcolm excused himself and started across the garden with the intention of joining Gregory Neville, the detective story writer, but he was intercepted by the pair of tall young Germans, who seemed to materialize before him, wreathed in warm smiles and glowing with good humor.

The taller of the two said, "May I introduce myself? I am Willie Maganer. Permit me also to introduce my friend, Karl Webber."

In turn they shook Malcolm's hand in the continental manner, a single up-and-down motion as precise as the stroke of a piston.

"Later we would like to speak with you," Willie Maganer said. "It's too early now, too soon after the event, but may we call on you one morning this week?"

"We would appreciate it greatly," Karl Webber said warmly.

"All right. I'm at the Pensione Royale."

"Yes, we know, Mr. Malcolm," Willie Maganer said.

They smiled at him, bowed courtesouly, and moved off to mingle with a group at the opposite end of the garden. Malcolm went over to join Gregory Neville who stood alone looking into a glass of punch with an expression of suspicion and wonderment on his long cold face.

"Mr. Neville, may I speak to you a moment?" Malcolm said.

"Please do, by all means," Gregory Neville said, sniffing discreetly at the punch. "Do you know what they put in this stuff? It smells like a sort of pudding we were given as kiddies at Christmas. Currant jelly with a tablespoon of

72

port on it. Quite vile, really. Do you suppose there's any whiskey about?"

"I don't think so."

Neville sighed and sipped the punch. Then he looked questioningly at Malcolm. "You wished to speak to me?"

"Yes. You mentioned that you write detective stories."

Neville glanced warily at him over his glass of punch. In the depths of his cold blue eyes flickered a cautious interest. "You like detective stories, is that it?"

"Yes, very much," Malcolm said untruthfully. "Do you write any other kind of fiction?"

Neville's smile became icy. "No, I write only detective stories, young man. I do not call them novels of ratiocination, or novels of violence, or novels of any other sort. Neither do I call them 'entertainments,' as one of our eminent authors prefers to when he deserts God for the nonce to do a bit of potboiling. He wants the Prize, of course, so he's on a precarious tightrope. Will the Nobel Committee overlook one last thriller, for instance, if he follows it up straightaway with an abstruse and pretentious essay on the Albigensian Heresy?" Neville put his punch glass aside with a precise gesture, wiped the last traces of the offending liquid from his lips with a handkerchief, and then smiled frostily at Malcolm. "In short, I'm not respectable. Isn't that what you wish to know?"

"Of course not," Malcolm said hastily. "I'm terribly sorry if I gave you that impression. The thing is, I'm trying to write a detective story myself. And I was just desperate enough to hope that you might give me a little help with it."

"I see. I imagine you've tried epic verse. the theater, legitimate novels and the like. Having found these unsuited to your talents, you've decided to tackle detective stories, a form that any clod should be able to master in the odd weekend or so. Is that it?" Neville's smile was weary, but beneath his elaborately sardonic manner Malcolm sensed a wrath so intense and a bitterness so painful that he was touched with pity for the man.

He was tempted to retreat into soothing banalities, and withdraw from this lacerated ego; he didn't care to know what publications had never reviewed Neville's books, nor what unkind things had been said to him by callous editors or more successful writers.

Neville said, "You mustn't put me down as just a waspish crank. But people have a habit of patronizing detective story writers. I can't see why. It's decent, honorable work,

73

and it takes a great deal of thought and preparation to do it well."

"I'm sure of that," Malcolm said. "Also I'm sure you're bored to tears by amateurs who want to tell you their plots."

Neville was not completely mollified, but there was a bit more humor in his expression. "No, the worst of amateurs is that they *have* no plot. Neither do they have characters, background, or any knowledge of what's been done in the field, and what can't be done in the field."

"Exactly. That applies to me. I don't have a plot, just a vague area of interest."

"Which is?"

"Guns," Malcolm said.

"Smuggling?" Neville made the criminous connection instantly and effortlessly, like a spark leaping from a negative to a positive field.

"Why, yes," Malcolm said.

Neville nodded thoughtfully. "It's a line of country pretty well posted by Ambler, you realize. But there are always changes to ring. What sort of guns?"

"I hadn't given that much thought."

"I suggest you give it a great deal of thought," Neville said in pedantic accents. "If you write up a lot of nonsense about guns, the reader will put you down for an ass, and your book down with a bang, half finished. First of all, hand guns and shoulder weapons would present you with totally different problems. In packing, in shipping, in expense, and so forth. Further, they serve different purposes. Now think of the various weapons available to you. Lugers, Springfields, Enfields, Garands, Savages, Winchesters, Remingtons." Neville paused to draw a deep breath. "Then consider machine guns," he went on, with the pleased air of a man who has unexpectedly been given an opportunity to display an obscure expertise. "Classic examples are the Chauchat light machine gun used in World War I, and the various Mauser shoulder rifles developed in Germany. Later we came along with the Maxim and the Vickers, and you Americans perfected the Browning heavy machine gun, an illustrious advance, needless to say. We followed with the Besa 15 millimeter, and the Germans introduced an exceptionally fine lightweight, which I believe they classified as MG 42. There were, of course, the British Sten, the Australian Austen, and the German Volksturm Geschuss, which translates rather charmingly as the People's Shooter. Interestingly, that gun was chambered for the same high-powered cartridge—"

"Yes, I understand exactly," Malcolm said, interrupting him as gently as possible. The noise of the party and the pleased drone of Neville's voice were giving him a headache.

"Then I suggest you decide on a specific weapon, and do some homework on it." Neville said. "Now: where do you propose to find these guns? What use will they be put to? And what country do you propose to smuggle them into?"

"Oh, into Spain," Malcolm said quickly.

"That might be interesting to think about," Neville said, and drew a pipe from his pocket with a slow, deliberate gesture, which, in the light of his occupation, was as significant as that of a knight buckling on his sword or a housewife rolling up her sleeves.

"I'd like to tell you something about the characters," Malcolm said, in an attempt to forestall another encyclopedic barrage.

"Never mind your characters," Neville said shortly, and began to pack his pipe. "Characters aren't my forte. At least it pleased the *Times* to declare as much in their Christmas issue several years back. Puppets—fascinating, cleverly maneuvered, but still puppets, alas!"

Neville applied a match to his pipe, the flame revealed points of pure malice in his eyes. "And that, in all probability, from some proudly unclean young man with half a sordid novel tucked away under his bed. Never mind the characters. But I'll give you a hint or two on where your problems will crop up. Getting the guns into Spain! That should provide a neat challenge to your ingenuity. I'd suggest you find an up-to-date map and go over it with a magnifying glass. Take a sharp look at the French and Portuguese borders. Unless you bring them in by sea, France or Portugal will be your likeliest line of country." He smiled and poked his pipe at Malcolm. "Short of tunnelling under the Mediterranean from Africa, or devising some complicated air-drop operation, you've got just the two alternatives—land or water. And let me give you a last word of advice. Do please remember ammunition. Half the gun-smuggling tales I come across seem to ignore that little detail completely. Guns galore, packing cases full of them, but never so much as a round of ammunition in sight. The authors must expect the rifles to be used as clubs."

This notion set Neville to laughing so heartily that several of the guests turned to stare at him. Malcolm also laughed heartily, and Neville whacked him on the shoulder in a comradely fashion, rewarding and encouraging him as he might an appreciative pupil. When he finally recovered from this paroxysm of hilarity, Neville wiped his eyes and said to Malcolm, "Just one or two points about ammunition now."

And until the candles guttered and died, and the last guests were leaving, technical terminology flowed as steadily and remoreselessly from the Englishman's lips as bullets from a machine gun.

The policeman of Cartama had been interested in Tani's account, but dubious of its reliability.

"Now Don Fernando demands to know much more," Tani said helplessly to Malcolm. "Who is buying the guns from Domingo? How is he going to smuggle them into Spain? Where are they coming from?"

"I think Don Fernando might do a little work on his own," Malcolm said. He hadn't hinted to Tani that the information he had given her was based on a series of guesses, to which a gloss of authenticity had been applied by a British detective story writer. The situation seemed mildly amusing to him, and he smiled as he thought of the plump little policeman stalking his office and wrinkling his brow in an attempt to ferret out the secrets of the phantom guns.

Malcolm was lying on the couch in Tani's room, with only a cotton sheet covering the lower half of his body. It was early in the evening, not dark as yet, and through the windows he could see the light of the fishing boats moving slowly out to sea. The fishermen would row out a mile or so, drop their long nets, and then patiently row back to shore to haul their catch from the water. It was a hard night's work; at first light in the morning they would still be hauling on the ropes that pulled the big nets through the bitterly cold sea.

Tani sat on the arm of a chair watching him with a hopeful smile. She wore only a slip and when she drew on her cigarette the glowing tip cast a gentle light on her bare shoulders and arms.

"Can you find out more for me?" she asked him.

"Probably."

"Then I could go away." She hesitated a moment, looking at him wistfully. "Have you thought of something else?"

"What?"

"We could both go away."

"Tani, come over here," Malcolm said.

She sat beside him on the couch and ran her fingers lightly

over his bare chest and shoulders. "Couldn't we be happy?" she asked him.

"You wouldn't recognize happiness if it ran you down like a truck. Neither would I."

There was just enough light in the room for him to see her face. She stared at him steadily, impassively, but her dark, lustrous eyes seemed full of pain. "We could be happy," she said, in a childishly stubborn voice. "You don't have to kill anyone. Domingo can't make you do it."

"That's right. I don't have to do it. He can't make me. And that's why I will. It's free gesture."

"But it makes no sense."

"That's why it's free. It's a gratuitous, meaningless act of violence. If it were otherwise, it wouldn't be free." Malcolm patted her arm. "Don't try to understand it."

She shook her head slowly, and he saw the tears flashing in her eyes. "No, you mustn't do it. Domingo wants to make an animal of you. It's what he likes to do to everyone. He is a pig and he can only be happy in a world of swine. Don't you see that?"

"This has nothing to do with Domingo," he said. "Please stop talking about it. We can be happy for a while. Can't you accept that? And stop worrying about whether you'll be happy next month or next year."

"I'm afraid for you," she whispered.

"Do you want to be happy now?"

"Yes, I do," she said, in a soft helpless voice. "Please."

At first Tani had insisted this wasn't necessary. In fact she told him it wasn't possible. Too much had been done to her without love. She elaborated the meaning of this in clinical detail, hoping to spare herself any pointless tenderness. She couldn't enjoy a man, now or ever, not after having fought down her responses so long just in order to survive. She had trained herself to study her wrist watch, to think of clothes she might buy, to plan week-ends along the river, while her body had suffered an infinite variety of mechanical assaults and abasements. It had finally meant nothing at all to her, and in the first week of her relationship with Malcolm she had been exasperated by his attempt to overcome the leaden coldness of her body. She couldn't accept his gentleness, for there was nothing within her to hold warmth or passion, no receptacle to contain any emotion but disgust or indifference.

But Malcolm had refused to believe her. With a confidence and understanding he had never known before, he had worked on her as skillfully as a locksmith would on the tumblers of a vault, until finally he had discovered the combination of timings and touch and pressure which made her responses spasmodic and liberated her emotions from the domination of her will. At first she had been terrified of this sweet agony. There was something fearful in the ascent to that quivering equipoise of pain and pleasure. For nothing could save or protect that subtly straining balance; it was doomed to die of its own violent aspirations.

But the real miracle to Tani was that this death led only to a new life.

Yet Malcolm knew something which she would never know. Her responses had nothing to do with the mechanical technique of his attentions and caresses. They had failed from the start. And then he had deliberately willed himself to love her unimportant body. It was a meaningless act, as empty and worthless and free as the murder he would commit for Domingo. But it was that which had moved her so powerfully, the simple illusion of love. It was sad and funny, but the truth seemed to be that the more preposterous the illusions, the more easily people could be convinced that they were real.

Tani lay beside him, her body as slack and languorous as something made of silk, and laughed gently at her memories.

"You were very good to me," she said.

"Why are you laughing?"

"I don't know."

"Once I heard a story about a lovely young woman who would be kind to anyone who could make her laugh. Do you know that story?"

"Please, I don't like that story."

"Was it true?"

"Please don't talk about it," she said unhappily. "I don't want to remember that day."

"Was the story true?"

"Does it matter? No one comes here now. Only you. I have sent Jorge away. I need no one but you now."

"Was he your bodyguard?"

"Why do you want to talk about it? To me it's like nothing happened until you came here. Can you believe that?"

"Did Jorge make you smile?"

"He wouldn't dare to touch me," she said, with a flash of anger. Then she rubbed her cheek against his shoulder, ashamed of having spoken that way to him. "Please don't talk about it any more," she said gently. "I don't know if the story was true. Maybe it was. I was afraid I might forget how to smile. Can you understand that?"

"Yes, of course," Malcolm said smiling.

"Stay with me," she said, whisperpering the words against his bare shoulder. "Don't do what Domingo wants."

"Now you're talking like a fool, Tani."

She put her dark head on his chest and began to weep like a weary, frightened child. She wanted to go away with him, to make him happy somehow, but she knew in her lonely heart that there was nowhere on earth where they might rest in peace and fulfill her dreams.

10

THE two Germans, Karl Webber and Willie Maganer, occupied a suite high in the Pez Espada, a luxurious hotel on the edge of the fashionable town of Torremolinos. Their sitting room and bedroom opened on a balcony which provided a view of the sea and the wide beaches which curved toward the distant city of Málaga.

Karl and Willie escorted Malcolm into their suite with an air of charming solicitude, as if they considered it a pleasant but serious responsibility to have someone so fragile and precious entrusted to their care. They had called for him that morning at his *pensione,* and had driven him back to their hotel in a blue Porsche which clung to the curving mountain road as if it were on tracks. The day was brilliant and sunny, the whitecaps frothing in a stiff wind, and the two Germans had seemed like caricatures of high, vigorous spirits with their flaming cheeks and sparkling blue eyes, their colorful, cablestitched sweaters and soft leather walking shorts.

They were associate professors at the University of Frankfurt, in the Department of Psychological Studies, working under the direction of Professor Albrecht Altheimer. This they had explained to Malcolm on the way to the hotel.

There were dozens of books piled about on the tables

in the sitting room. The suite was pleasantly cluttered with metal filing cabinets, luggage, a motion picture screen, and several vases of fresh flowers. On the terrace, a pair of cable exercisers hung neatly on the balcony railing.

Karl was the older of the two; light streaks of silver glinted at his temples, but he gave an impression of indestructible youth with his fine clear eyes and skin, and the supple, powerful lines of his body. Willie was less grave, less ponderous than Karl. Although he was as powerfully built as his companion, there was more elegance and grace in his movements, and his high coloring and charming smile lent a certain boyishness to his manner.

Together they symbolized the traditional images of Nordic virility and innocent manly pleasures: undergraduates chanting songs in beer halls, marzipan and hot chocolate on frosty nights, fräuleins in bright dirndl skirts running breathlessly from laughing young men in a green park, duelling clubs, and the music of country fairs and travelling circuses in the springtime.

"I am sorry that you aren't familiar with some of the work Professor Altheimer has done in the field of confessional therapy," Karl said, as he led Malcolm to a comfortable chair. "Of course, there's no reason you should be familiar with it," he added with an apologetic smile. "It's all highly technical, and probably dry as dust to anyone outside our field. The professor has lectured in your country, at the universities of Pennsylvania and California, and published several books there. One of these, *Schizophrenia and Its Inducement Through Fear and Hysteria* achieved the distinction of making a little money, which as you know is rare in the field of scholarly publishing."

Willie picked up the telephone and smiled at Malcolm. "Would you prefer tea or coffee?"

"Coffee, thanks," Malcolm said.

After ordering three pots of coffee, Willie pulled a chair over and sat down facing Malcolm. The two Germans regarded him with smiling approval.

"It is so good of you to give us this time to talk to you," Karl said.

"Yes, you are most kind, most considerate," Willie said, and then his smile became slightly mischievous. "Not to say courageous."

"We are doing research and experimentation with what you might call crash analysis," Karl said, emphasizing the last two words with an earnestness that bordered on solemnity.

"To drive at the truth of human motivation with accurate, rapid strokes, that is our goal. Normally a deep analysis requires three or four years. But the psychiatrist knows the ultimate destination of this long journey in a matter of months, sometimes weeks. The patient, of course, fights the truth about himself, out of fear and guilt. He uses mechanisms of repression, displacement, selective aphasia, to defend himself against seeing the truth. The doctor, in a sense, must encourage him to remove the dark glasses from his eyes. And this is what takes so much time, because the patient is afraid to look at the painful memories of his past. This is true, even under hypnosis."

"We are experimenting with techniques which may lead the patient directly to the truth about himself," Willie said, with another charming smile at Malcolm. "This is why I salute your courage. The early formative years of any person's life are the most significant, for it is within that framework that one's sense of security and personal worth are most strongly determined. If you cooperate with us, we will have to ask you a number of painful questions."

Malcolm said, "Then you'll tell me why I offered to kill myself for a glass of brandy?"

"Yes, I think so," Karl said.

"Very well, fire away," Malcolm said.

"I think an illustration might demonstrate clearly what we are attempting to do," Karl said, and glanced inquiringly at his companion. "The Belgian?"

"Yes, the Belgian is an excellent example."

"This was a case of hysterical blindness, no physical reason for it whatsoever," Karl said to Malcolm. "A Belgian, call him Etienne, thirty-five years of age, who was on holiday in Frankfurt. One day he became blind. Like that!" Karl snapped his fingers. "Without warning, with no previous symptoms of eye trouble. He was brought to our clinic, and we learned his background: Etienne was unmarried, one of two children, the second being his older sister. Etienne's father had died a few months after Etienne was born. His mother was a resourceful, vigorous woman, with a good business head. She kept her husband's business running. It was a small pottery factory near Liége. Etienne's sister married and had seven children. Etienne stayed home and helped his mother take care of the factory. Then Etienne's brother-in-law came on difficulties. He lost his job and went to Paris to try to find another. To ease their circumstances, Etienne's mother took in three of the smallest children and provided for them. This arrangement lasted for nearly a year. Etienne was like a father to the three youngsters. He took them on holidays, heard their lessons, prepared them to receive their first Holy Communion, and so forth. Last year, Etienne took a trip to Frankfurt, and blindness struck him without warning."

"Like that!" This time it was Willie who snapped his fingers. "We guessed at the source of his trouble immediately, and a few talks with him confirmed our first tentative diagnosis. As a child without a father, he had become inordinately dependent on his mother. Naturally enough, he would have fantasies of marrying her, and later he would dream of sleeping with her, of becoming her husband. This must have become a fixation with him, one which produced powerful feelings of guilt counterbalanced by fears of losing her. Inevitably, he never married. He must have tried to force his feelings of guilt, and corresponding self-hatred, below the limen of his conscious mind. It was the arrival of the children in the home which touched a match to the fuse. The physical similarity to a family undoubtedly became dreadfully apparent to him. So long as he was a bachelor he had been successful in suppressing his guilt. But when he became his brother-in-law's surrogate, a father by way of position and authority, his unconscious desires for his mother became unbearably severe. And so his defenses broke. He fled from the scenes which intensified his needs, and his corresponding self-hatred. There was only one solution—to blot out the world he found so detestable, so humiliating to look at. And so he unconsciously willed himself never to see it again."

"And what happened to Etienne?" Malcolm asked him.

"The pity of it is, we don't know," said Karl with an unhappy smile. "We had no authority to tell him our conclusions. The shock of facing the truth might have destroyed him. On the other hand, it might have allowed him to see and understand his situation without such corrosive anxiety."

Willie said. "The truth about mankind, as Jung tells us, is not in our history books, but in all the clouds of myth and superstition and imagery which are gathered in the human unconscious. To part those clouds is to reveal the truth, but unfortunately, this has always been a lengthy process."

"And so we are back to where we started, at crash analysis," Karl said. "To give you a last example, there is a prosperous businessman in Frankfurt who cannot open a door." He smiled somewhat anxiously at Malcolm, as if apologizing for this seemingly whimsical or irrelevant state-

82

ment. "It is almost funny. But it is, in fact, quite tragic. In the evening his wife or the maid must be waiting to open the door of his home. Otherwise, he would spend the night in the street. If he were in a burning building, he couldn't save himself if it meant turning a doorknob. This much we know of him: as a young child during the war he lived on a street where a dreadful atrocity occurred. A Jewish family lived in the house opposite his. Soldiers came one night and pounded on the door of their home. The father refused to open it. The soldiers hammered on it with the butts of their rifles. It was a thick, solid door, and it took them a long time to break it down. Our patient watched all this, and when the door was finally smashed open, the sixteen-year-old daughter of that Jewish family jumped from her window into the street and was killed. Our patient saw this too, but he refuses to remember it. So far we have not been able to lead him back to this scene. But the linkages are clear to us: he is, himself, now married to a woman who is half-Jewish, and whose health is not good. Unconsciously, he resents the fact that she is part Jewish, and unconsciously, he despises himself for this disloyalty. Behind the clouds that veil his unconscious mind, there are massive guilts. He tries to save his ill wife—as he couldn't save another helpless Jewish girl—by refusing to open any doors. Further, he punishes himself by choosing a sentence that makes him look both pathetic and absurd."

"We hope to find techniques to alleviate such symptoms more quickly than is possible now," Willie said. "Our patient may be led to an understanding of his anxiety in two or three years. We would like to spare him, and others, such cruelly long exposures to pain."

Malcolm settled himself more comfortably in his chair.

"Do you smoke?" Karl asked him, extending a package of Craven A's in his clean, massive hand.

"No, thank you."

"May we commence then?"

"Sure, let's go," Malcolm said.

The questions about Malcolm's early background took the rest of the morning. Karl interrogated him while Willie made rapid notes on small white cards. The questions related to his father and mother, his religious training, his attitudes toward animals, schoolteachers, and friends.

"Did you cry easily as a child?" Karl asked him.

"No," Malcolm said.

Karl glanced at Willie. "Tears constitute only a part of

the defensive pattern, so please make a note to compare the negative response with the Psychogalvanic Reflex."

"Of course," Willie said.

Karl smiled apologetically at Malcolm. "This must be confusing to you. If you have any questions, please feel free to ask them."

"I'd rather answer yours," Malcolm said.

"Perhaps that is better," Karl said, and proceeded with his interrogation.

Malcolm suspected all this would prove pointless. He couldn't in honesty provide these serious and likeable young men with a chamber of horrors from his past. He had grown up in the country around Ridgefield, Connecticut, and his father, a contractor, had taken him gunning every day of the open season. The woods were thick with small game—rabbits, pheasants, groundhogs, and squirrels; and Malcolm and his father always got their limit, which distressed his mother greatly, for she was forced to pluck the birds and dress the game which her brave hunters heaped so proudly on the kitchen table. Malcolm's mother was a slim, pale woman with no very compelling interests beyond the condition of her garden and greenhouse and the welfare of her family, which consisted only of Malcolm and his father.

Malcolm mused on the fact that he had once been a fairly good shot. It was odd to think of those long autumn afternoons in the fields as training for the debt he owed Domingo. And he wondered what his father would think if he could possibly have known that he was preparing his son to kill a stranger for a glass of brandy.

Malcolm had been raised in a comfortable home surrounded by comfortable ideas. When he found that many of these weren't true, such as virtue being its own reward, for instance, he had been relieved, for he had suspected early in life that many of the things his father and mother told him were embarrassingly unrealistic. In the many schools he had attended, from the age of five to twenty-one, he had learned only that the middle of the road was the safest place to walk, unless there was heavy or dangerous traffic, in which case it might be wiser to take to the fields.

Karl and Willie did not indicate that they found any of this information trivial or insignificant. They were as grave and attentive as priests, and the little stack of white index cards grew higher and higher as Malcolm talked on.

"Now you must tell us of your wife," Karl said with a sympathetic smile.

Malcolm had married Jane Cordwainer when he was twenty-eight. She had admired his background (which was properly upper middle-class) and also the snapshots of his prosperous relatives which filled the family albums. The pictorial record of his family was an apotheosis to an enviable American Way of Life, with its rows of elm-shaded streets, large homes, polished cars, and all the flushed and smiling faces gathered about at formal weddings or ski lodges or patio cocktail parties.

Janey had wanted for all this, and so she had married him. He hadn't been particularly eager about the idea, the sexual congress being one he had never campaigned for with much vigor. Certain of his physical needs embarrassed him, and in repressing them he had achieved a passivity in sexual areas which extended just to the borders of impotence. But to his relief and surprise, Janey felt very much as he did about such things, and they had effected a satisfactory adjustment with only intermittent and well-ordered deviations from their customary state of affectionate physical neutrality. And since Janey was an animated, vivacious, and attractive girl, and Malcolm was tall and rangy, with a handsome face and muscular body, it was assumed by everyone that their tolerant and confident manner toward each other in public must be grounded on private intimacies of a deep and powerful nature. They were given credit, in short, for being profoundly and seriously in love, with the result that women stopped making passes at Malcolm, and men sighed wistfully but hopelessly over Janey, convinced that all of her needs were being attended to with jealous and sedulous care by her devoted husband.

This suited them both very well. They enjoyed sun bathing, skiing, work, and travel, and nothing would have upset the delicate balance of their schedules more than flirtations and affairs. But they never discussed this, for it was difficult to put a complacent attitude toward continence into so many words.

Yet now, with Tani, his passions flowed as naturally from him as water from a mountain spring. There was no fear of failure, no guilt, no reluctance to investigate any roads which might conceivably lead to pleasure.

As he related these curious facts, Willie's gold pencil raced faster and faster over the index cards, and Karl looked out at the sea and stroked his chin with a thoughtful gesture.

"Your wife was ambitious?" he asked Malcolm.

There was a little child inside Janey Cordwainer, a child who had grown up poor in a drab Midwestern town and hadn't gone to the one proper school or played tennis at the country club. Oh, yes, she was ambitious. Janey would go anywhere on an assignment, but the thrill for her wasn't the bizarre excitement of distant lands, but the chance it gave her to send exotic postcards to all her friends back home. The little boys and girls who had gone to dancing classes and music recitals were proper burghers and matrons now, and Janey used postcards like venomous darts in an attempt to puncture their self-esteem and composure.

She never saw any of these people when she was in the United States. Wild horses couldn't have dragged her back to that little town with its absurd pecking order, but she was grimly and maliciously determined to let everyone there know when she bought a dress at Dior's or covered a flood in Nigeria.

At this point Karl switched his interrogation to the area of Malcolm's political convictions and his attitudes about various world leaders.

They ate an excellent lunch of cold shrimps, thick, tender filets, grilled tomatoes, and fresh asparagus. After dessert and coffee, they returned to work.

Willie took Malcolm's blood pressure, and Karl checked his pulse and peered into his eyes with a pencil flashlight. They looked into his mouth and struck his knee with a rubber-nosed hammer.

During the afternoon, he was exposed to sections of the Berenreuther Personality Inventory, Rorschach Test, Thematic Apperception Test, Stanford-Binet Intelligence Test, and the Pintner-Patterson performance scales.

In addition, he studied various shapes which Willie constructed quickly and skillfully on the coffee table from small, oddly-angled blocks of wood. He explained which designs he liked and which he didn't, which made him feel cold and which made him feel warm. A revolving wheel threw patterns against the walls, and he was asked to decide which patterns were friendly and which were unfriendly.

With the lights out and the shades drawn, Malcolm studied pictures of cloud formations on the motion picture screen. None of them seemed menacing to him, and this reaction— or lack of reaction—caused Willie to stare at him anxiously.

Karl explained the functions of the galvanometer as he placed the small black metal box on the table before Malcolm. The machine had a metered face, and two electrodes attached to electric cords.

"This may be mildly uncomfortable," Karl said, but he smiled reassuringly as Willie taped the electrodes to the palms of Malcolm's hands. "Only a pinprick or so, actually. The psychogalvanic reflex describes the changes in the electrical properties of your body. We are going to make you experience certain emotional reactions, and the meter readings will indicate the ohmic resistance of your body under emotional stress."

"Are you ready?" Willie asked him with a smile.

"Yes."

They stuck pins into his forearms, shouted abrupt warnings into his ears, slapped him lightly but unexpectedly on the cheeks, and called him abusive names in excellently simulated tones of contempt and anger.

"You have been a very good boy," Willie said, laughing breathlessly, as he removed the electrodes from Malcolm's hands. "But now we are through, that is the last of it."

"Would you like some tea?" Karl asked him anxiously. "Or a whiskey, perhaps? I know it has been a fatiguing day for you."

"No, thank you." Malcolm watched Willie as he collected the heap of index cards and placed them neatly into three narrow metal containers. "You've got the answer there, is that right?"

"Yes, I think so," Karl said. "With our computers at the University we would have it in five minutes. But it will take us several days to organize and analyze this data." He smiled at Malcolm. "But believe me, the true profile of your personality exists in these little stacks of cards."

Willie laughed and slapped his companion lightly on the seat of his soft leather walking shorts. "And we'll find it, if we have to work all through the night." And then he turned to Malcolm and said, "You must forgive my enthusiasm, but it is something we feel each time we add a case history to our files. We are that much closer to our goal. There are many unhappy people in the world who unfortunately have the power to make others unhappy through their own fears and anxieties. Think of the results if we can perfect techniques of crash analysis to apply to neurotic labor officials, to statesmen and dictators, to owners of newspapers whose guilty needs make them publish lies and distort the news!"

"This dream is a long way off, of course," Karl said, smiling indulgently at his companion's flushed cheeks and sparkling eyes. Then he winked at Malcolm. "I am content only to break ground, but Willie here will not be happy until the beautiful edifice we dream of becomes a reality."

"When will I get the results of these tests?" Malcolm asked.

Karl looked at him seriously. "You wish to know our conclusions?"

"Why, yes."

"Very well," Karl said quietly, and with a certain resignation in his manner. "If that is what you wish, in two days, three at the outside, we will stop at your *pensione* and tell you what we have learned."

They would learn the truth as they were able to understand it, Malcolm thought, but they wouldn't understand the real horrors they had snared and caged in those narrow metal boxes of index cards.

11

THAT same night Clarke, the Englishman, came to Malcolm's room. "Domingo wants you," he said.

The smoke from the cigarette stuck to his lower lip curled up slowly about his gray face, and blurred the look of cautious cruelty in his gray eyes.

Malcolm felt shock running through him in a series of steady, rhythmic jolts; but it wasn't fear, he realized, it was anticipation. He smiled at Clarke. "Is this the night I pay for that drink?"

"It's the night he wants to see you," Clarke said. "That's all I know."

They drove up to the Arroyo de Miel in Clarke's Citroën, an *onze leger* with Gibraltar registration plates. The night was cold but the drifting winds were soft as velvet on Malcolm's cheeks. He could smell the scent of the geraniums growing beside the curving road. Malcolm tried to decide how and what he was feeling now, because it seemed to him that anything he perceived at this moment must possess some especial significance; but he found himself thinking about nothing at all, although he had read somewhere or other that such a thing was impossible. He was aware of Clarke's sullenly silent presence beside him, the wind on his face, the scent of flowers, and that was all.

Domingo's bar was crowded with fishermen but the poker table was empty, the green felt cover shining dully in the bright overhead light. Clarke led Malcolm into a room behind the bar, in which were a sofa, hollowed out like a hammock from Domingo's great weight, and a desk covered with dusty bills and correspondence. They continued down a flight of stairs to a dimly lighted corridor whose brick walls were slick with moisture. After they had walked along for twenty yards or so, Malcolm noticed that the surface of the walls had changed; instead of brick, it was of roughly hewn rock, and he realized that they were in a tunnel hacked into the side of the mountain behind Domingo's bar.

Clarke led him through an open door into a room hollowed unevenly out of the rock and lighted by a naked bulb hanging from the dripping ceiling It was apparently a storage area; heaps of fish-netting and cordage and cases of brandy and beer were stacked against the walls.

They left this room and entered a narrower tunnel, and after about ten yards came to a closed door made of thick, solidly braced slabs of wood.

Clarke knocked twice and the door was pulled open a few seconds later by Domingo. The Frenchman's huge body filled the doorway, and the light behind him threw his mountainous shadow far down the tunnel. He stared impassively at Malcolm for an instant, and then sighed wearily and struck him across the face with a hand as thick as a two-by-four and wide as a ping-pong paddle.

"Bring him in," he said to Clarke, who was smiling with satisfaction as he supported Malcolm's sagging body in his arms....

The cavelike room which had been hacked out of the dripping rock was about the size of the Germans' hotel suite, Malcolm judged, when his eyes finally came into proper focus. Except that the ceiling looked to be about ten feet higher. He sat in a chair against the wall facing the single door of the room, while Domingo paced back and forth before him with the lumbering gait of a caged bear. There were a few chairs about, and a low table was shoved up against a thick wooden beam which served as a brace for the ceiling. The single electric bulb threw a harsh, yellow cone of light onto the floor, and the corners of the room were in shadows.

Clarke stood by the barred door in a negligent but watchful posture, with a cigarette glowing from his lips in the gloom. He was looking at Malcolm, almost, but not quite, smiling.

In a corner of the room, almost lost in the shadows, an elderly man sat erectly in a straight-backed chair, his hands resting on the top of a cane. He wore a wide-brimmed hat, and Malcolm could see the gleam of his polished, ankle-high boots in the murky light. There was a suggestion of brooding intensity in the rigidity of his body, and while he sat in profile to Domingo, his head seemed cocked appraisingly to the sound of the Frenchman's heavy restless footsteps.

A knock shook the door and Clarke raised the heavy rod which barred it. When he pulled open the door, Paco came sprawling into the room, propelled from behind by a powerful shove from Zarren.

Domingo lifted Paco to his feet by the lapels of his well-cut jacket, and shook him so savagely and relentlessly that the young Spaniard's head snapped back and forth as if his neck were broken.

Zarren came into the room and Clarke barred the heavy door. Paco was screaming softly, and his cries of entreaty were so splintered and shattered that they sounded as if they were being shaken from his body by Domingo's hands. Finally, Domingo threw him aside as he would a filthy rag, and strode back to where Malcolm sat against the wall.

"You talked to him about the guns, eh?" he said, bending down to shout the words into Malcolm's face. "You lie to me, I'll kill you."

Malcolm began to laugh. "Sure I talked to Paco about the guns," he said.

The anger faded slowly from Domingo's face. He stared incredulously at Malcolm. Then he scratched his huge, cannonball of a head with a gesture of almost plaintive bewilderment.

"He admits it," Domingo said, turning to stare at Zarren and Clarke. "You hear him? He admits it."

The old man sitting in the shadows shifted his position slightly, and Malcolm saw dark eyes staring at him from the blurred rectangle of a weathered face.

"Ah, he's clever," Clarke said. "He guessed straight away. I heard him and Paco at the party, clacking like bloody hens."

Domingo turned back to Malcolm. "You know he heard you?"

"No, but I might have guessed it," Malcolm said. "He's the sort you usually find with his ear at half-open doors."

Clarke spat a stream of filth at him.

"Or at keyholes," Malcolm said, smiling.

"Where did you find out about the guns?" Domingo said quietly.

Malcolm nodded at Paco. "From him."

"He's lying," Paco said in a trembling voice. Struggling to his knees, he stared imploringly at Domingo. "He is lying. Don't believe him. I swear before God, I swear on my mother's honor he lies." Paco's eyes bulged piteously from their sockets, and all his love of life, love for the breath in his lungs and the blood coursing through his slim body, was nakedly revealed by the fear and agony in his straining features.

Domingo shrugged and looked at Malcolm. "So he calls you a liar. What of that?"

"The woman he sleeps with has a daughter. Paco bragged to her about getting rich, and made a joke about the guns. The little girl didn't understand what it meant. She told me, and I guessed at it."

Domingo frowned at him. "Just guns, that's all you know. Nothing else?"

Malcolm shook his head.

Domingo looked down at Paco's kneeling figure. "And the American pig you sleep with? You tell her, too?"

"I told her nothing, I swear it."

"But you told the child, eh?"

Paco's eyes were glittering with tears. He moaned helplessly and said, "I only made a joke with her. She understands nothing."

Domingo turned and looked at Malcolm with an embarrassed smile. He shrugged uneasily, and said, "I'm sorry."

"I'm not interested in your guns," Malcolm said. "I'm not interested in you, either."

"I know that, I know that," Domingo said quickly. "It's all right." He patted Malcolm's shoulder in a clumsy gesture of apology. "It was my fault. You and I understand each other. Everything is all right between us." Then he turned and began to pace back and forth before Paco's huddled figure, staring down at the Spaniard's dark glossy head with an expression of impersonal repugnance.

He looked as if he had noticed a bit of filth on the floor, and was clinically disgusted with it.

"You just made a joke, eh?"

"Yes," Paco said weakly.

"So everything's fine now, everything's all right. Is that what you think?"

"It didn't mean anything. It was only a joke."

Domingo rubbed his jaw thoughtfully. "Paco, a joke is a matter of opinion. What one man thinks is funny, another man may not. You understand me?"

Paco looked up slowly, a cautious hope flickered in his eyes, for Domingo was smiling, and there had been an indulgent tone in his voice.

"Yes, I understand," Paco said quickly.

"And this joke with the child, you think that was funny?"

"It was meant to be funny."

"You must be amused then." Domingo prodded him with the toe of his shoe. "Let me see you smile. Let me hear you laugh."

Paco tried to smile, but the effort only twisted his face into a grimace of terror.

"That's better," Domingo said. "Now laugh."

Paco began to laugh, softly and tentatively, as if this were a difficult task he was attempting for the first time, but as Domingo smiled and nodded approvingly at him, Paco's confidence expanded and his laughter rose in volume until the sound of it bounced frantically against the rocky ceiling and walls of the cave.

Domingo was smiling, and so were Clarke and Zarren; only Malcolm and the old man in the shadows did not smile.

Finally Paco stopped to catch his breath. He sat huddled on the floor sucking air gratefully into his lungs. Occasionally he laughed weakly and helplessly, as if he were being prodded by the memory of an unbearably amusing situation.

Domingo stopped smiling and his face became cold and expressionless. He looked at Malcolm and said, "You owe me for a drink."

"You want it now?"

Domingo took a revolver from his pocket, inspected the cylinder critically, then extended the gun, butt first, to Malcolm. "Settle your account," he said, and jerked his head toward Paco. "Kill him."

Malcolm took the gun from him and got to his feet. "You mean this?" he said quietly.

"Kill him," Domingo said.

Malcolm stood with the gun hanging limply at his side, trying, as he had tried on the drive up the mountain with Clarke, to analyze his thoughts and feelings. But there was nothing inside him, it seemed; it was as if all his emotions and reactions were in a deliberate and willing state of suspension.

Malcolm raised his arm and pointed the muzzle of the revolver at Paco's forehead, and the silence in the room suddenly became oppressive and smothering. No one seemed to breathe. Clarke held his cigarette an inch from his gray lips, his eyes flicking between Malcolm and Paco, while Zarren stepped back a pace and crossed himself with a gesture that seemed as helpless as it was involuntary.

Paco began to whimper softly and the sound trembled against the heavy silence, as pathetic as the flutter of a bird's wings on the bars of a cage. He knelt directly under the cone of yellow light which fell from the naked electric bulb, his black hair shining with lustrous health, and his hands locked so tightly over his mouth that the words he tried to speak broke into cracked, inhuman noises against his trembling fingers.

The old man stood slowly and watched Malcolm with a mild appraising smile.

Domingo looked closely at Malcolm. "You had a drink, pay for it."

Paco screamed like a woman.

Malcolm aimed for a bead of sweat gleaming on his forehead. He increased the pressure of his finger, and saw the strain slowly whiten the knuckles of his hand.

When he pulled the trigger, the dry click was like a thunder clap in the straining silence.

Domingo began to laugh boisterously. "You can do it, you will do it," he cried, and his eyes blazed with admiration and affection as he pounded Malcolm's shoulder.

Paco fell forward limply and helplessly, as if whatever had been holding him upright had suddenly been severed by the blow of an ax. He lay on the floor, clawing weakly with his fingers at the rocky floor, while queer, liquid noises strained deep in his throat.

"You don't want me to kill him?" Malcolm asked Domingo.

"We will arrange that," Domingo said. "But it was necessary to know you could do it. I have no more doubts."

"This was just a game then," Malcolm said quietly.

"A very serious game."

Malcolm smiled at him. "But I knew the gun wasn't loaded."

"No, you couldn't know that," Domingo said, shaking his head slowly. "You never looked at the cylinder."

Domingo was right, Malcolm realized; he hadn't known, he had only guessed that the gun wasn't loaded, feeling quite certain they wouldn't kill poor Paco anywhere near the Arroyo de Miel. He glanced into the cylinder of Domingo's gun and saw the dull gray noses of five bullets gleaming in their chambers. The chamber in line with the barrel was empty now, of course.

Almost of its own volition, it seemed, the gun in Malcolm's hand swung slowly back and forth across the room, and the arc it described enclosed the four men who stood watching him in silence.

"You'd better make sure, Domingo," Malcolm said, and smiled at the frown gathering on the Frenchman's face.

"But I am sure," Domingo said in a puzzled voice.

"I knew you were playing games. Take my word for it. You proved nothing. Shall I kill him now?"

"No," Domingo said.

"Then who do you want me to kill?"

The room seemed suddenly cold, and Paco's whimpering sobs died away in his throat. He stared with glittering eyes at Malcolm.

"Don't talk crazy," Domingo said, but something in Malcolm's pleased smile tightened the frown on his face. "Don't be foolish," he said, in a quiet and reasonable voice. "You don't have to kill anybody tonight. We understand each other. I know you will do it when I tell you to."

"Supposing I kill you," Malcolm said thoughtfully, and while his tone was pleasant, the smile had faded from his face and the light above him revealed the emptiness in his eyes. "You taught me what I'm worth. You bought a ticket to my execution for a glass of brandy. But you also taught me what you're worth. So why cling to life? I can assure you it's not worth it. Do you want to go on drawing one breath after another until the blubber around your heart kills you? Think honestly, Domingo: do you really want to live?"

"Put that gun down," Domingo said hoarsely.

"You had better answer my question. I'm quite serious."

Domingo wet his lips. "Yes, I want to live. Give me the gun now."

"Then supposing I kill Zarren?"

"Don't kill anybody, you crazy fool."

Malcolm glanced idly at Zarren. "Do you want to live?"

Zarren moved forward and the cone of the yellow light falling from the ceiling coated his bald head and blond mustaches with gold.

"Yes, I want to live," he said, quite formally, but with no suggestion of appeal or concern in his manner.

"Tell me why."

"My brother is in Poland. He is old and sick, and there is no one to care for him. I am looking for money so I can return to Warsaw and bring him back with me. Until he is free I would prefer to live."

"I pity you," Malcolm said. "When his health is better and he is living comfortably off you, he will blame you for not helping him sooner and more abundantly. You will sit alone in cafes drinking down his ingratitude with your schnapps."

"It will not be like that," Zarren said quietly. "And now it is I who pity you."

"Okay then, what about Clarke?" Malcolm smiled at the small Englishman. "How long has it been since you enjoyed a meal? Or a woman? What bright dreams are keeping you alive?"

Clarke threw his cigarette aside with a contemptuous gesture. "Shoot me and be done with it, if that's what you want," he said in a savage whisper. "But spare me your bleeding lip."

"I'll oblige you then," Malcolm said, but even as the gun swung about slowly, Clarke flattened himself against the wall and shouted frantically, "For God's sake, don't. Please don't shoot."

"Then supposing you tell me your reasons for wanting to live," Malcom said dryly. "Do you hope to captivate some lovely heiress and sail away to lotus land on her yacht? Or win one of the soccer pools and spend the rest of your days drinking pink gins in front of the telly?"

Clarke's small gray face was shining with sweat. He shook his head helplessly. "I want a room with a lock that a sledge hammer couldn't break. I want to hide there and think of the thousand places where I left part of me forever. You wouldn't understand, none of you could," he said in a voice that was bitter with shame. "But it's as good a reason for living as any other."

The old man in the shadows said quietly, "Have you considered me?"

"Not until now," Malcolm said.

The old man moved into the light and regarded Malcolm with an inquring smile. He was tall for a Spaniard, almost six feet, and he wore the loose trousers and short jacket of a stock breeder. There was a flash of rough lace at his throat, and his leather boots had the luxurious glow of well-kept silver. Under the wide brim of his flat-topped hat, his eyes were deep and dark in sockets lined with a filigree of wrinkles. He was in his early or middle sixties, but his long, well-shaped face was firm and brown, and his quietly hanging hands looked capable of a hard day's work in the fields.

"My name is Gonzalo," he said. "I work as foreman at a ranch where bulls are bred. I am a friend of Domingo's, and I stopped here for a glass of wine while the owner of the ranch I work at does business in Málaga. All of these are good reasons for killing me. Or allowing me to live. It depends on your view of such matters."

The old man's eyes were clear and quiet and steady and Malcolm looked into them with a little thrill of recognition; something intimate lurked in their depths, and Malcolm had the sudden exhilarating conviction that this old man knew and shared his secret. Something in his smile and manner told Malcolm that they were the only true conspirators in this room. They had both been exposed to the ultimate lie or ultimate truth of existence, and so this old man would know that whatever happened here now was of no more significance than the spilling of a glass of wine.

"We owe someone a death," Malcolm said, and tossed the gun to Domingo. "Whether I kill you, or you kill me, it doesn't matter. We're only spilling the cheapest liquor in the world."

Domingo stared at the gun as if it had materialized in his hands through black sorcery. "You want me to kill you?" he asked Malcolm in a thick, stupid voice.

"Why not?"

Domingo moved slowly toward Malcolm. He approached him tentatively and almost fearfully, as if he suspected that this man who stood smiling quietly at him possessed mysterious, unnatural powers and might be protected by legions of baleful, invisible demons.

He studied Malcolm's smiling face with an expression which represented an almost comical blend of affection and apprehension.

"I believe you," he said at last.

And then Domingo began to smile, too, and his smile was so tender and grateful that his whole personality seemed transformed by its gentle radiance. He put his gun away and patted Malcolm's shoulder clumsily and respectfully, and his eyes were moist with emotion as they roved hungrily and proudly over Malcolm's face; it was as if he were regarding a cherished son who had only now returned safely from long and dangerous campaigns.

"All my life I have waited for you," he said gently. "Without knowing, I have been waiting for you. You are the strength I have always wanted. You will be ready when I need you."

"Yes," Malcolm said.

Everyone watched him as he walked to the door. There was no sound in the room. Clarke opened the door with a gesture of ironical servility, but the effect was marred by the fact that he couldn't quite make himself meet Malcolm's eyes.

Only the faint wheeze of Paco's labored breathing accompanied Malcolm's footsteps into the damp tunnel.

12

ONE brisk morning in the following week, Gregory Neville, the British detective story writer, hailed Malcolm in the square of the village. He seemed in far better spirits than he had the night of Coralee Davis' party; he wore slacks, a baggy wool sweater, and there was color in his cheeks from wind and sun. Even his bushy brown mustache had undergone a sea change of sorts; it looked perky and luxuriant, flaring under his long, cold nose like twin pennants of healthy exuberance.

"I've been giving your problem some thought," he said, smiling a bit sheepishly. "Busman's holiday, that sort of thing. I couldn't get your illicit guns off my mind."

"Fine, let's have some coffee."

They sat at a table on the deserted terrace of the Bar Seville. "I came on this at a shop in Torremolinos," Neville said, taking a soft-cover book from his pocket and handing it to Malcolm. "Memoirs of a German colonel who served with Rommel in the Afrika Korps. It's clotted with the usual *mea culpas* after the fact, and so forth. But it does contain some interesting material on shoulder weapons. You might find it worth while to look at."

"That's very thoughtful of you," Malcolm said.

"Not at all. Now here's what I suggest," Neville said briskly. "Imagine your problem this way."

Malcolm watched sadly as Neville removed the tools of his trade from his pocket, a stubby pipe and a well-worn leather tobacco pouch.

"You'll need a good supply of guns for one thing," Neville went on expansively, after he had gotten his pipe belching and fuming with satisfactory intensity. "Ridiculous to insult your readers' good sense by raising a fuss over a dozen-odd rifles or so. No, pick a large but manageable number, say five hundred or a thousand. Secondly, choose good sturdy weapons which don't require ordnance experts to put and keep them in order. I thought of your own Garand first, but it isn't likely there's any of those about for your villains to pinch. Would you think so?"

"No, I wouldn't think so," Malcolm said.

"Of course not," Neville said, acknowledging this good judgment with a smile. "Then I stumbled on something in the colonel's memoirs. I'd forgotten about it myself, but the Germans experimented in World War II with a shoulder weapon very similar to the Garand. It was semiautomatic, gas-operated, quite a fine rifle altogether. It was classified Gewehr Model 41, and there were two modifications, the 41 W and 41 M. They were chambered for the standard German rifle cartridge, which was 7.92 caliber." Neville folded his arms and regarded Malcolm with good-humored challenge. "Where do you imagine a supply of those Model 41's might be found today?"

Malcolm looked thoughtful for an appropriate moment. Then he said, "I really don't know."

"Put on your thinking cap, old boy," Neville said. "Algeria!"

"Algeria?"

"It's completely logical. Thousands of Model 41's must have been lost during Rommel's various retreats. Who'd be most likely to find these abandoned guns? Berbers, Arab tribes, and so forth. In the perfectly dry desert air, these rifles could pass white-glove inspections for years."

"Absolutely," Malcolm said with an emphatic nod.

"Now imagine calendar leaves flipping over the way they

do in films. The years pass. We come to the trouble in Algeria, the revolt of the army, the long years of guerilla fighting. That's when our Gewehr Model 41's came on the scene again. From caches and caves all over Algeria, they were hustled into action, whether for profit of patriotism doesn't matter two pins to your story. The thing is, the guns must still be there! The rebels never surrendered with their arms, if they could help it. They hid them away in the hills, ready for the next go-round of Palace disorders.

"Now supposing some adventurous chap stumbled onto them, say for example, a soldier of fortune who'd been messing around in Algeria." Neville's excited smile conferred equal professional status on Malcolm; it suggested they were getting on nicely, hammering their ideas into precise and interesting designs. "I do think we're putting some flesh around the bones of your yarn," he said.

Clarke came out of the Bar Seville and stood on the terrace, his narrow shoulders hunched against the cold. He had drunk two small glasses of rum, and there was a faint trace of color in his gray face.

"But how am I going to get the guns into Spain?" Malcolm asked Neville.

"After all, old boy, it *is* your story," Neville said, but his air of exasperation was only meant to be amusing; he was obviously delighted to display his occupational skills. "I'll give you one tip on that point, for what it's worth," he said. "This is based on personal experience. I've got some dour old relatives in Scotland, and I occasionally go up there to tramp about the moors. Rinses off the smoke and grime of London very effectively, I find."

Clarke lit a cigarette, flipped aside the match and started for the sidewalk. Then he noticed Neville and Malcolm sitting with their heads together at the far end of the terrace. He paused briefly, anger streaking through him like a current of electricity, and then he turned and walked over to their table.

"I'd like to talk to you," he said to Malcolm.

"Why, of course," Malcolm said. "Do you know my friend, Gregory Neville?"

"No," Clarke said.

Neville's eyebrows rose slightly in response to the blunt dismissal in Clarke's tone and manner. He glanced up and took a cool inventory of Clarke's gray, pinched features, the cigarette hanging from his lips, the ill-cut suit which gave an impression that it hugged the frail body of its owner with certain reluctance. Then he said pleasantly, "Won't you join us, old man?" in a manner which suggested that he had been raised from birth to show kindness to all of God's creatures, regardless of what odd shapes and sizes they came in.

Clarke sat down defiantly, but his body was as stiff as that of a dog being pulled toward a master holding a switch.

"Mr. Neville writes detective stories," Malcolm said to Clarke. "Do you like detective stories?"

"No more than any other kind of fairy tales," Clarke said.

Neville regarded him with a kindly but puzzled smile; it was the way he might have reacted to an assertion that the earth was flat. "You must find a friend to read one to you," he said, with such sympathy that Clarke winced as if he had been flicked with a whip. "It might be an amusing experience."

"I can read the bloody things myself," Clarke said sullenly.

"Really?" Neville's eyes were fixed on an invisible point just above Clarke's left ear. "You must forgive me, old man. The thing is, one tends to forget how Labour broadened the educational base, doesn't one?"

"The thing is, you don't know damn-all what you write about," Clarke said contemptuously, but his eyes were bright with anger and frustration, for he knew that no words of his would ever penetrate the wall of glacial indifference Neville had so effortlessly raised between them. "You write about murder like it was a tea party. Do you know whether a man squeals or grunts or screams when a knife goes into him? Or what a head looks like when it's been smashed by bullets?"

"Good heavens, no," Neville said calmly. "I don't believe in murderers. Any more than I believe in the Loch Ness Monster or Abominable Snowman. They may very well exist. There's evidence for it, to be sure. But I prefer to dismiss it as unreliable. Philosophically, I think of knives and bullets as obeying the laws of physics, rather than the impulses of men. If I knew any real murderers, I couldn't write about them as I do."

"It would be my pleasure to put you out of business," Clarke said, with the smile like quicksilver running across his gray lips.

Neville glanced at his watch. "We must talk about this again. It's frightfully interesting. But would you mind awfully if I finished what I was saying to Malcolm here?" He shifted his chair an inch and caused Clarke to cease to exist. "We were talking about Scotland, weren't we?" he said to

Malcolm. "Yes. The weather was too foul for any outdoor activity, so I was confined to a rather gloomy houseful of drafts and portraits of distant ancestors, most of them churchmen. I decided to make the best of it, and plot out a new detective yarn. But it came slowly. I was thinking of a London background, and I couldn't quite imagine that setting while surrounded by dripping trees and foggy moors. Then I had an inspiration. I discarded London altogether, and transplanted my basic plot to a dreary old house in Scotland. Things started clicking beautifully then. I called the book *Murder, in a Manor of Speaking.*" He smiled at Malcolm. "Pun, you see. And it was well received, I must say."

Neville finished his coffee. "The moral is, take advantage of your immediate surroundings whenever possible. If I were you I'd forget about the French and Portuguese borders. Use what's at your fingertips."

"The village of Cartama?"

"Precisely. It's as unlikely as any other area of Spain, but there's the fun of writing 'tec novels. You can perform the impossible with a few strokes of a pen."

He shook hands with Malcolm, smiled at Clarke as if he were surprised to find him still present, and then hurried off down the street, the wind blowing sharply through his bristling mustaches.

"Bloody bastard," Clarke said frowning after him. "What's worse? Sticking a man with a knife, or treating him so he wants to stick you with a knife? To him I'm ignorant scum, and he enjoys letting me know it."

"He's getting back at you for treating him like a lord," Malcolm said.

He looked up at the mountains above the village. Rain was falling slightly and thick masses of fog were drifting like smoke down the hills. The air was damp and cold on his face.

"Listen to me," Clarke said quietly. "Domingo's stalling. He's got a feeling about you that makes me want to vomit. But when he gives the go-ahead, if you muck your end of it, I'll make bloody damn sure you never get another chance. Maybe that won't bother you. You're already more dead than alive. But you'll be all dead when I'm through with you. Just remember that!"

Malcolm continued to stare at the mountains. There were whitewashed farms standing in gray squares of tilled land, and olive trees that looked no larger than pine cones stuck up and down the slopes.

"I told you to listen to me," Clarke said, and put a hand on Malcolm's arm.

"Yes, of course. I remember. Something about killing me." Malcolm glanced at him with a warm smile. "It's all you people seem to think about. But if you do, one night there'll come a tapping on the locked door of your room. You won't want to answer it. You'll try not to. But something will force you out of bed and make you cross the cold floor to unlock that door and open it."

Clarke watched him with a grin. "You're coming back to haunt me, is that it? Wrapped in a bed sheet and rattling your chains." He laughed softly. "Save your ghost stories for the kiddies. I haven't met the dead man yet who could give me a turn."

Malcolm stood and looked up and down the street. The day was growing darker, and the rain water was collecting in the gutters and pushing bits of paper and filth sluggishly along with it.

Clarke watched him anxiously. He laughed and said, "So who'll come tapping on the door to disturb my sweet dreams?"

"You won't see his face," Malcolm said, as he inspected the street with a critical eyes. He wanted to photograph this today; in the chill leaden air, with water trickling down the muddy walls of the shops and dwellings, there were certain things to see that were obscured by sunlight and brilliant skies.

"Who'll it be?" Clarke said in a queer, small voice.

Malcolm looked down at him and shook his head slowly. Then he smiled and left the terrace.

Three astonishing things happened to Malcolm in the course of that day.

The local priest stopped him as he was entering his *pensione* and begged him to leave the village. "You are a blasphemer, and you mock the lives of my people. Go away, please."

The cold wind from the sea blew the old man's thinning hair in erratic swirls about his head. A light burned in his worried eyes.

"I'm sorry," Malcolm said.

"You must take your corruption some other place. My people risk the contamination of their faith. They know what you have done, and they see you rewarded for it. The village doubts God's justice."

"I promise I'll leave, Father," Malcolm said. "But there's a job I must do first."

He gently removed the old man's clawlike hand from his sleeve, and entered his *pensione*.

Then, as Malcolm came up from the beach much later in the day, a fat and untidy American girl stopped him and struck him in the face with the palm of her hand. She giggled as she backed away from him, and he realized that she was tight.

"You're a phony, I know it," she said, and put her chubby fingers over her mouth as if to suppress the laughter bubbling up in her throat. In the gloom of the early evening, he saw that her eyes were bright with tears. She backed away from him until she collided with the wall of a shop, and then, without another word, she turned and ran heavily up the street, her flat shoes striking the old stones with a sound of panic and fear.

The third astonishing thing was that Jenny Davis came to his room that night to tell him Paco was dead.

13

MALCOLM ate dinner with Tani. While she prepared the food he found himself thinking of the fat American girl who had struck him in the face, and with less interest, of the old priest who regarded him, it would seem, as a carrier of moral pollution.

What was that girl doing blubbering about the streets of a poor Spanish village? It made no sense at all, and this gratified Malcolm. The priest was another matter. There must be a hard core of self-interest at the heart of the old man's concern, and thinking of this only fatigued Malcolm.

Tani placed a casserole of chick peas, sausage, and pimientos on the low table, lit candles, and poured two cups of tea.

During dinner he told her that Domingo was attempting to smuggle five hundred German rifles into Spain from Algeria. This whole business now seemed a highly original joke in Malcolm's view. But it was a serious sort of joke, he had decided. For it was obvious to him by now that all human behavior was supported or justified by one sort of fiction or another.

But when he finished his account, Tani shook her head miserably.

"I can't remember all those guns and numbers," she said. "I don't want to."

"You want your passport?"

"Yes."

"Then concentrate on a few simple facts. Never mind the Gewehr Model 41 and its modifications. Just think of German rifles. That's point one. Point two, they're in Algeria. Point three, they'll be smuggled into Cartama somehow, sometime."

She stood and walked to the window and stared at the darkness. "It's crazy, it's dangerous," she said. "I don't want to know any more."

In a white dress and high heels she looked unexpectedly tall and slim against the frame of the dark window. Earlier she had seemed happy. There were fresh flowers in the room, and the bracelets on her slim wrists flashed and sparkled as cheerfully as the lights in her dark eyes. But now her face was miserable.

"I'm afraid," she said. Then she turned and looked at him pleadingly. "Why don't you go away from here?"

"Aren't you happy now?"

She sat down on the sofa and smiled helplessly at him. "Yes, right now I am."

"Why not just enjoy it then?"

She shuddered and locked her hands together in her lap. "I can't stop worrying about what will happen."

"Then you're a fool."

"I'm not a fool," she said so forcefully and stubbornly that he couldn't help smiling at her. "You can laugh, I don't care," she said, stung by his expression. "But there are times when you make me feel like I did when I was a little girl. When I would put on a clean dress and sit before the fire to wait for my mother to come home. It was in Paris, and the apartment was tiny. I tried to be so quiet that I could hear the clock ticking in the kitchen. I told myself that I was a very good little girl, and that my mother would be so happy to find me waiting for her. Sometimes you make me feel that way again. And I can smile when I think of myself."

She had spoken of things it hurt her to remember; tears

were in her eyes. "I'm not a fool to worry about what will happen. Don't you see that?"

Malcolm stood and sat down beside her on the couch. "Let's don't talk about it any more, okay? Did you know that Paco is dead?"

"No, please!" She barely whispered the words, but the alarm blazed in her eyes as vividly as the flash of a lighthouse in a storm. "Did you—" She stopped abruptly and stared at him with an expression blended equally of fear— yes, there it was, the thought—and fascination.

"No, I didn't kill him," he said. "He ran off the road up in the mountains. He and his shiny motorcycle fell into a canyon. His body was discovered only a few hours ago. They think he was drinking."

"Who found him?"

"Domingo."

"It was an accident," Tani said weakly. "It was only an accident."

"In a way I suppose it was," Malcolm said.

He believed this. He didn't feel responsible for Paco's death. Paco had died for a world that was no more meaningful or significant than the one which Gregory Neville had created for Tani. He had boasted of wealth to little Jenny Davis. He had amused himself by creating an exciting world for her, one in which he stood laughing and bowing at the footlights. And these charming wisps of fancy had grown into serpents which strangled him.

Tani was afraid, he realized. She snuggled close to him, and he felt the tremors in her slim body. Frightened of shadows and phantoms.

"Let's be happy now," he said.

"No, I can't."

He was almost touched by the curious logic of her fears; for worry over the future, she would sacrifice this real pleasure.

"Yes, you can," he said.

He had that authority over her. In the illusion of love he created, it was possible for Tani to think of herself and what she had been with a tolerant smile. And she needed forgiveness for herself more than the air she breathed.

The following morning she told the policeman everything she could remember about the guns. Don Fernando listened without comment and without expression, but occasionally he made a pencilled note in a report book on his desk.

Outside, it rained steadily and the sky was the color of putty, but the policeman's office was as warm and humid as a greenhouse, with heaps of cherry-red charcoal glowing in two brass braziers, and all the windowsills and door jambs chinked with strips of green felt against drafts. It was a small room, containing only Don Fernando's desk, two chairs, a filing cabinet, a framed map, and a picture of the Generalissimo.

Tani sat in a straight-backed chair facing Don Fernando across his desk. She tried to judge his interest from his expression, but so far her account had only creased his forehead with a faint frown.

When she finished speaking, Don Fernando sighed as if a nearly insupportable burden had been placed on his shoulders. He leaned back in this chair and stared at the ceiling.

"German guns, eh? Big Berthas, perhaps? Or water pistols?"

"He gave me some names and numbers," Tani said anxiously.

"Would you be so kind as to give them to me?"

Tani rubbed her forehead and tried to remember all the confusing terms Malcolm had mentioned to her. "It was something like Model 41," she said at last.

Don Fernando removed his gaze from the ceiling and looked steadily at Tani. His eyes narrowed, as he considered her last remark. "The Model 41 was an experimental rifle which the Germans used in Africa, as a matter of fact," he said slowly. "How many rifles are there, Tani?"

"Five hundred."

"I see. And how are they to be brought into Cartama?"

Tani shook her head helplessly.

"You don't know?"

Again she shook her head.

"It's an amusing tale. Contraband rifles. Desperados smuggling them over deserts. I'm surprised you didn't invent camels and a love story." He walked to the window and stood with his back to her staring at the gray sea. "Where did you read all this?"

"I'm telling the truth," she said desperately.

"You expect me to believe such nonsense?"

"I can't make you believe it. I can only tell you what I know."

"As I say, it's very amusing."

Don Fernando laughed softly, but there was a tight, cold pain in his stomach. The narrow path he was travelling toward safety suddenly seemed knotted with dangerous curves. The very floor beneath his stout boots seemed slippery and uncertain; one false step and he would plunge to destruction.

Supposing it were all true, he thought anxiously. Should he turn this information over to Madrid? They would send alert, hard-eyed men down to deal with it. Yes, he thought gloomily and they would give him no credit at all. He would continue to direct traffic and see that beach shorts weren't worn in the village after five o'clock and never taste the fruits of victory. But never mind that. It was the zealots, the thirsters for glory, who always got their heads cracked with the next swing of the pendulum.

But if he didn't notify Madrid, how could he explain that later?

"Why would I lie to you?" Tani said wearily and hopelessly.

"Because you fear me. You hate me. You might be telling me a pack of lies to get me in trouble. Or make a fool of me."

"I only want my passport so I can go away."

"Be silent. I must think."

He might lie to Madrid, Don Fernando thought; deny that he had had any advance information of Domingo's plans. The policeman breathed easier; yes, that was safe. Or he could report that he had come on the plot accidently, and had taken immediate steps to crush it. And *that* would be safe, if events went the other way. The insurgents—if there *were* insurgents—would have only themselves to blame for not taking him into their confidence.

Don Fernando turned to study a framed map of the Mediterranean coast which hung beside the portrait of the Generalissimo. He located the city of Algiers, and let his eyes rove slowly down the shoreline to what had formerly been Spanish Morocco. The port town of Ceuta would be a logical point of embarkation, he decided; it was directly across the sea from Cartama.

Without looking at Tani, he said, "The American. He tells you he will kill someone for Domingo, eh?"

"Yes."

"Not for money?"

"No."

"He doesn't know who. Or why. Correct?"

"Yes," Tani said helplessly.

"Please don't go on insulting my common sense," he said frowning at the map. Ceuta, it must Ceuta, he thought. "Even a stupid American is not that stupid, Tani. To kill someone for nothing. Someone he doesn't know. For no reason at all. It is ridiculous. You must find out his victim. And you must find out how the guns are to be brought to Cartama."

"Then you will let me go?"

"If you are telling the truth."

He resumed the restless pacing behind the desk. There was a policeman in Ceuta he might call, Manuel Hernandez. If Manuel knew that rifles were being brought into old Spanish Morocco, he could sniff them out.

But this posed a delicate problem. He had no place in his budget for telephone calls outside the country. To write a letter was an alternative, but he dreaded putting such sensitive information on paper. But a long distance call would cost several hundred pesetas, and inevitably some sharp-eyed clerk would notice that item while auditing his accounts, and there would be a dozen forms to fill out explaining and justifying the expense. And if the guns actually were coming from Ceuta, what ominous interpretations might be placed on his unauthorized call there?

He sat down and pressed his fingers against his throbbing temples. "I am not well," he said in a straining voice. "I am sick. And it means nothing to you. Leaving here, it's all you care about."

"I have tried to help you."

Don Fernando's problems were suddenly illuminated by a brilliant inspiration. As he examined them in this fresh burst of light, his anger and frustration diminished. He smiled at Tani. "Yes, you have tried to help me," he said. "But I require further assistance now."

He removed a yellow tablet from his desk drawer, and took a pen from an ink well with the crisp, fussy gestures of an experienced bureaucrat.

"You have come to me with a problem," he said. "Quite properly, since I am the constable of Cartama. It seems you lost some valuables in Ceuta a month or so ago." Don Fernando nodded and began to write in a neat rapid hand. "Yes, exactly. A valise. Left in a taxi, or perhaps taken from your hotel room. You didn't report it to the police because—" He stopped and frowned at the ceiling. After deliberating a moment, he smiled and continued writing. "There wasn't time, of course. You had to catch a bus or train, something like that. Now you have come to me for help. You wish me to call the police in Ceuta and make inquiries for you." He looked blandly at Tani, who was frowning at him in bewilderment. "The difficulty is, I have no budget for such calls. If we extended such services to all tourists, we would have no money left for anything else. But if you can pay the charges—three hundred and fifty pesetas will cover them—I will make the call to Ceuta." Don Fernando's schizophrenic transformation seemed complete; he smiled neutrally at Tani, tendering her the assistance of his rank and office with impersonal and disinterested courtesy.

"You want three hundred and fifty pesetas?" Tani said dubiously.

Don Fernando shrugged. "It's up to you, of course."

Tani sighed and removed three bills and two coins from her change purse. The policeman counted the money carefully, placed it in a cash box in his desk, and entered the amount in a ledger. Finally he wrote a receipt and gave it to Tani.

Now everything was in order. When his superiors in the provincial administration queried him about the call to Ceuta, his answers would be supported appropriately and disarmingly by many spools of red tape.

"You may go now," he said and picked up the telephone.

As she stood and turned to the door he watched her guiltily; she wore slacks and a thin gabardine jacket, but they didn't conceal the smooth swell of her hips and breasts, and even the damp curls at the nape of her neck caused lewd, forbidden images to drift before his eyes.

When the door closed behind her, the policeman rubbed his forehead slowly. In keeping her here, he was literally playing with fire.

He breathed a prayer and resolved to let her go.

Then he told the distant inquiring voice in his ear that he wished to speak to Manuel Hernandez.

14

THE central plaza of Cartama was growing dark when Malcolm came down the road from the hills. Rain blew about in erratic bursts. He had his hands in his pockets and his Leica safely inside his zippered-up windbreaker.

The burros going home brayed rhythmically and stoically as the winds snapped at their coats. The terraces of the cafes were empty and the table tops were mirror-slick with rain water.

Malcolm had had a telephone call from Gregory Neville earlier that afternoon.

"Hallo? Hallo." Neville's voice had been a jovial shout; it was as if he hoped to triumph over an uncertain connection by sheer volume. "Malcolm, are you there? Can you hear me? It's Neville here!"

Malcolm held the receiver a few inches from his ear; the connection hadn't been that bad.

"Yes, I can hear you perfectly."

"Good!" Another great shout. "I'm in Marbella, on my way to Gibraltar. It's been a lovely holiday. I enjoyed Spain thoroughly."

"That's fine."

"I stopped here for tea, and couldn't resist ringing you up. Driving along the coastal road, I came on the answer to your problem. Getting them into Spain, remember? That's where we ran dry, wasn't it?"

"Yes."

"Very well. I'll give you a hint. Then let's see if you can work the rest out for yourself. Go to the beach early tomorrow morning and have a good look about. If nothing clicks, ring me at the Queens Hotel in Gibraltar and I'll put you onto a solution to your problem. Fair enough?"

"Yes, of course."

"I must say, I've enjoyed our talks, Malcolm. Quite frankly I hadn't counted on the opportunity of talking shop in Spain. It helped pass the time marvellously. Now one last tip: this is a bit of professional secret—don't feel obliged to make all your clues relevant. If the story sags here or there, run a blood-stained handkerchief or a torn railway ticket into the thick of it. If it turns out they weren't significant, who's likely to care? Keep things popping. And please remember what I told you about ammunition, 7.92, that's what those Model 41's are chambered for, you'll recall. So have plenty of it about. But most important, go to the beach first thing in the morning, and keep a sharp eye on everything that happens. Will you do that?"

"Yes, of course."

"Then if you don't ring me in Gibraltar, I'll know you

saw exactly what I did, and that you're homeward bound with a steady wind in the sails. All the best, old man."

When Malcolm put down the receiver he decided to walk up into the hills and take some photographs. Somehow, he knew that the time for such diversions was about over.

Now, drenched and tired, he started across the plaza to the street which curved down to his *pensione*. But he stopped when he saw a familiar blue Porsche parked behind the local bus, which was slowly ingesting a sodden queue of passengers for Málaga.

He walked over to the car and rapped on the rolled-up window. Through the streaming glass he could see the blurred outline of Karl Webber's handsome, blond head.

Karl cranked the window down and looked up at him with a brilliant, startled smile. He wore a dark leather jacket with a yellow scarf at the throat. The wind stirred his thick blond hair, and the dashboard light scored his classically moulded features with interesting lines and shadows. Except for an odd nervousness in his manner, he put Malcolm in mind of a figure from Norse legends about to set off on some cheerfully perilous mission.

"It is good to see you," Karl said, shouting the words as if he were trying to make himself heard over the roar of a storm rather than a drizzle of rain. He smiled widely and pointed to the empty seat behind him. "Willie is in the shop buying some wine and sausage for our trip."

"You're going away?"

"Back to work, I regret to say." Karl's smile was rueful, and he shrugged with an air of philosophical resignation, but for all these conventional indications of regret, it looked to Malcolm as if Karl were most eager to be on the way; the smile on his lips was strained, and his eyes roved about uneasily, touching everything in sight but Malcolm's. "And so we must cut short our stay in Spain," he said quickly. "We intended to write you from Frankfurt. After all your cooperation, we didn't wish to disappear like smoke in a wind. We are most grateful to you. But here is Willie! He will be pleased to see you."

Willie had appeared in the doorway of a shop carrying a large paper sack from which the neck of a wine bottle protruded at a jaunty angle. He put a hand over his bare head and ran to the car, laughing breathlessly. Malcolm opened the door for him, and Willie slid in quickly beside Karl, moving for all his great size as nimbly as a graceful girl.

"Thank you," he said to Malcolm, glancing up at him from

the depths of the car. "Very kind of you." For an instant, it was obvious he didn't recognize him; then his smile broadened, and he said, "What a wonderful surprise!" but there was an odd nervousness in his manner and the same air of anxiety which seemed to be emanating in almost palpable waves from his companions. "The holiday is over," Willie continued hastily. "We are returning to Frankfurt. It is lucky we have this chance to say *auf Wiedersehen*."

"Yes, Karl told me you were leaving," Malcolm said. "But I'm curious to know what you learned about me. What was the result of all those tests?"

"I'm afraid there wasn't time to organize and analyze the data properly," Willie said. "In Frankfurt, we will be able to use our computers and get immediate results."

"You mean you discovered nothing at all?"

"Very little," Karl said. "There wasn't sufficient time." They both smiled at Malcolm.

"We had some distractions, too, I must confess," Willie said. "Spain is tempting, you realize."

The interior of the small, powerful car provided a warm haven against the wind and rain, a snug retreat, fragrant with cigarette smoke and the tangy odor of expensive leather. Within this aromatic vacuum, Karl and Willie were crowded together as if for comfort or reassurance, and the fixed smiles they directed at Malcolm were like those of large, uneasy children.

"How about a cup of coffee for the road?" Malcolm said.

"No, but if you come to Frankfurt, please call us." Willie said.

"Yes it would be a great pleasure to see you," Karl said. He touched the starter with his foot. The motor caught instantly, and throbbed with a sound of silken power. "*Auf Wiedersehen!*"

Willie had been watching Malcolm with a sympathetic smile. Now he turned and put a hand on Karl's arm. "Please," he said, "I think there's time for coffee."

Karl sighed heavily and turned off the motor. He looked resigned and unhappy. "Very well," he said. "We will have some coffee."

They went into the warm interior of the Bar Seville and found an empty table. A stove glowed in one corner of the room, and the damp air smelled of coal smoke, tobacco, and wine.

Fishermen stood along the bar looking at the slow, heavy rain with appraising eyes. A table of French tourists were also contemplating the weather, but with gloom and suspicion, as if this were a misfortune designed solely for their discomfort.

Karl ordered coffee and sugar buns.

"They are very nice here," he said to Malcolm. "The ones with fruit inside are excellent. Do you take cream and sugar with your coffee?"

"No, thank you."

Karl and Willie exchanged questioning glances, and apparently reached a silent agreement on procedure, for Karl settled back in his chair, while Willie cleared his throat and moved closer to Malcolm.

"We did come to a conclusion about you," he said. "But it is quite tentative. Perhaps it is only an opinion. This is why we thought at first it would be wiser not to discuss it with you. It's difficult to put such matters in simple terms. To offer examples and analogies is not a very good solution. If one says, think of the mind as a tree, or a system of highways, or a wireless station, there's always the risk of creating misleading images and concepts.

"As you know, we attempted to draw a quick and accurate profile of your personality. To cast light on your hidden fears and needs. The results were quite—" Willie paused, glanced appealingly at Karl, then sighed and shrugged helplessly. "They were quite unexpected. To describe what we discovered about you, without shadings or nuance, I must rely on examples, images. Your responses are so unnaturally balanced that they completely contradict one another. Instead of emotional stresses and strains which interlock to support structures of coherent values, your mind presents us with a picture of quite logical, quite orderly chaos. Normally, a specific set of values will buttress those of the same class— in your case they cancel one another out in bewildering fashion. Certain responses shouldn't negate certain other responses—in your case they invariably do."

"The relationships are meaningless," Karl said, almost angrily. "The picture we drew of you was blank, absolutely blank." He pressed his fingers to his temples, and shook his head as if he were in pain. "We cast a light on your inner needs and desires, and the light reveals nothing. There is the chance we're wrong, you understand. That is why I didn't want to tell you these things. I haven't been able to sleep thinking of them. But Willie thought you had the strength to understand." Karl struck his forehead with the palm of his hand. "But *how* can he know? There *is* nothing to know."

Willie did not seem as distressed as his companion. He said eagerly to Malcolm, "Karl mentioned relationships. You recall the proximity tests?"

Malcolm nodded alertly.

"Very well. Consider the results. In a spatial relationship, your tests indicate that you are closer to heaven than to the devil; but closer to hell than to God. This is meaningless. It cannot be! It is pure chaos."

"It is as if you had never existed," Karl said in a low, miserable voice. "As if every impression made on you had been erased." He pushed the plate of sugar buns away from him with a gesture of irrelevant exasperation. "I'm sorry, I have no appetite."

"They're very good," Malcolm said. "Do you mind if I have yours?"

"Of course not," Karl said quickly. "Please help yourself."

"Mine too, if you like," Willie said.

"Thank you."

Karl and Willie watched with fascinated eyes as Malcolm devoured all the sugar buns with hungry relish.

Malcolm felt much better when he had finished the buns and drunk his coffee; his stomach was full, and the warmth from the coal stove was soaking pleasantly through his damp clothes.

He knew that Karl and Willie were uneasy. He saw the distressed glances flicking between them, the anxious smiles trembling on their lips. Malcolm regretted causing them pain and embarrassment, but he didn't know quite how to go about alleviating their apprehensions. Perhaps if he put on a little act it might help. Tore his hair, rolled on the floor, begged them for a word of reassurance or hope. But that seemed a lot of trouble for so simple a matter. And yet he knew he could never explain it to them. They believed, they were convinced, that they had come on something ghastly and unique—they would never understand they had only looked in a mirror. He decided the best he could do for them was let them escape.

"Well, you've got a long trip ahead of you," he said.

"Yes, yes," Karl said hastily. "Madrid by morning, it's a hard drive."

Malcolm accompanied them to their car. They shook hands with him gingerly, as if they wished they knew a way to perform this rite without actually touching him, and then they swung themselves into the stout blue car like a pair of well-schooled acrobats.

Malcolm waved good-bye to their blurred faces, and smiled after the car as it pulled away from the curb and bored into the rain that fell like a bright silver curtain across the plaza. The red taillights gleamed like frightened eyes in the darkness, and Malcolm stood watching them until they darted out of sight at the first curve in the road.

Malcolm became aware that a girl in a soiled white raincoat was watching him from the terrace of the Bar Seville. She was young and fat with oily brown hair tucked under a woollen cap. There was a suitcase at her feet, and she was obviously waiting to board the bus for Málaga.

Malcolm went over to her. "I'm sorry," she said, without meeting his eyes.

"But why?"

"I'm sorry I slapped you."

"Why are you sorry?"

"It was such a stupid thing to do. I had a few glasses of wine, but that's no excuse." She hesitated, and then added wild childish emphasis, "I'm sorry, truly I am."

"But why were you drinking?"

"I don't know," she said helplessly.

"There used to be a lot of Angry Jung Men in town," he said, and thought with pleasure of Gregory Neville's *Murder, in a Manor of Speaking*. "There's a pun in that," he said.

"I got it."

"Are you drinking because they've all gone home? Back to the Five and Zen cent store. There's another, by the way."

"Ha, ha," she said tonelessly.

"Why are you angry with me?"

"Because I'm fat," she said bitterly. "And because I'm going home. And because I can't write. And because my father, who owns the most progressive and imaginative hardware store in town, will call me his roly-poly little dreamer, and opine to his friends in the bowling league that he's glad I got quote all that nonsense out of my system end quote."

"I think I'd like him," Malcolm said.

"You spoiled it all," she said, and her face was suddenly flushed and swollen and ugly. "That's what you did."

Malcolm was touched by her unhappiness, but he had no words of comfort for her; there was nothing to do but leave her then on the cold terrace to wait for a bus to take her on the first lap toward home.

He walked down the dark street to his *pensione* in a very cheerful mood. For the first time in years, he felt like laughing at the black sky that was either man's blanket or shroud depending on his health, his bank account, and the songs he sang, or did not sing, in gonadic tetrameter.

For Malcolm had become convinced that the world was not as it seemed; and this struck him as amusing, although he knew in fact it was hardly a profound or funny conclusion. It wasn't that poor, dreaming, confused man—as he likes to represent himself—didn't know what he wanted; he knew only too well, and was afraid to take it. The world was a house of distorted mirrors, and everyone was running from the fearful sight of himself; and it must follow that all his ambitions and myths and religions were creations to justify that headlong, terror-stricken flight from reality to the shiny bits of broken glass at the foot of the rainbow.

No, it wasn't really so funny, he decided, but it would do until something funnier came alone.

At the foot of the street he met Tani, who was waiting in the dark at the entrance of his *pensione*.

She told him her unhappy news. "He wants to know how the guns will be brought into Cartama," she said wearily.

Malcolm remembered his telephone conversation with Gregory Neville.

"I have an idea about that," he said. "Let's take a walk down the beach."

"It's too cold and wet. Can't we go to my house?"

"Later," he said.

They walked about a quarter of a mile through the wet sand until they came to a cropping of rock which formed a lee from the wind and rain. They stopped here and Tani tried to light a cigarette, but the gusting winds snatched the flame from her lighter and sucked it away into the darkness. She threw the wet cigarette away and huddled close to him for warmth.

"Please, let's go to my house," she said miserably.

The rain fell heavily on their shoulders. Somewhere down the beach dogs were snarling over bones or dead fish. The lights of the fishing boats stretched like a string of diamonds on the horizon.

After a while Malcolm narrowed his eyes and frowned at the dark beach.

"Tani," he said.

"Yes?"

"You've been here in the morning, haven't you?"

"Yes, many times."

"Tell me what's it like then. Everything you can remember."

"There are people swimming. Men and women lying on the sand. Spaniards come with baskets to sell peanuts and fried sardines. The children play in the waves."

"Earlier than that," he said. "What's it like at dawn?"

"There are just the fishermen then," she said. "Everything is quiet, except for the singing as they pull in the nets."

"From Gibraltar to Málaga," he said slowly and turned to stare at the lighted boats far out on the water. "From Málaga north to Valencia, and north again to Barcelona, what attacks the coasts of Spain each and every morning of the year? What comes from the sea so consistently and inevitably that no one pays the slightest attention to them any more?"

She looked up at him with a puzzled frown. "The fishing boats? Is that what you mean?"

Malcolm began to laugh. "Think of it. Thousands and thousands of fishing boats beating inexorably against the shores of Spain since before the time of Christ. As punctual as the tides, as commonplace and unremarkable as the beaches themselves. An armada so blended against the background that it's literally invisible."

"I'm cold," she said, moving closer to him. "Why do you care about the boats?"

"That's how the guns are coming in," he said smiling. "Not in boats, but in the nets. It's so simple, only a genius would think of it."

That must have been what Gregory Neville had urged him to look for. The fishing nets, of course. Twenty feet long, six feet wide, each might hold several crates of rifles. There would be a rendezvous a mile or so off the coast; the guns from Algeria would be transferred to the nets of fishing boats, and the fishermen would then row them placidly to shore.

Now this should certainly satisfy the policeman, Malcolm thought. How could he doubt the authenticity of a plan so gorgeously plausible and ingenious?

"Are you only guessing?" Tani asked him.

"Far from it. This is the deal, trust me. Now let's go and get warm."

They took a cab from the village up to the Arroyo de Miel, and were happy there for a while. When he was ready to leave, she gave him the pink shepherd dog which stood guard over the tiny plastic sheep on the low table.

"Please take him," she said smiling. "He'll watch out for you. Then I won't worry."

15

PETER Kelly, the American sub-consul for the Province of Málaga, came to Malcolm's room at two o'clock that same morning.

He introduced himself and apologized for waking Malcolm.

"That's all right. What is it?"

"I'd like to talk to you."

"Fine, come in."

"Thank you." Kelly wore a damp gabardine topcoat, and drops of rain glinted in his red hair. While Malcolm pulled on a robe, Kelly shifted his weight from one foot to another, as if his tall rangy body were an awkward package he was trying to keep in balance.

"Miserable weather, isn't it?" he said, frowning absently about the small room.

"Would you like a drink?" Malcolm asked him. "Or I could manage a coffee if you have time. The landlady's daughter is very obliging about such things."

"No, please don't put yourself out," Kelly said quickly.

He seemed embarrassed and nervous, but it was obvious that he was trying to establish a properly serious atmosphere for whatever was on his mind; his frown had become solemnly intense, and he was studying Malcolm as a coach might study a player he was planning to send into a tight game.

Finally he said, "Don Fernando came to talk to me about you some time ago, Mr. Malcolm. He was worried about your conduct here in Cartama."

"I can imagine."

"You were drinking heavily?"

"All I could get my hands on."

Kelly cleared his throat nervously. "I have a serious reason for discussing this. I hope it's not too painful a subject."

"Not at all."

"You've stopped drinking, I gather."

"Yes, the road I was travelling suddenly seemed dull and uninteresting."

"You're serious about that?"

"Absolutely," Malcolm said. "I saw another road, a broad highway blazing with hope and promise, and I knew it led to glory. And so I took it."

Kelly looked at him skeptically. "Have you quit drinking for good, Mr. Malcolm?"

Malcolm smiled at him. "How could that possibly matter to you?"

Kelly rubbed his hands together and drew a deep breath. "It's just this: an American woman named Coralee Davis committed suicide a few hours ago. She emptied a bottle of sleeping pills and never woke up. You know her daughter, Jenny?"

"Yes, of course. Is she all right?"

"She's taking it very well, which is the idiotic phrase we use at such time. Too damn well for a child, if you ask me. She's poised, dry-eyed, composed, but that may be the quiet before the storm. I've placed a call to the States for her father." Kelly shrugged helplessly. "Meanwhile, however, Jenny refuses to stay at the *pensione,* and refuses to come back to Málaga with me."

"She wants to stay with me, is that it?" Malcolm said.

"How did you know that?"

"I don't know. I imagine I assumed it from your interest in my present character. It's all I could think of to explain it."

"As a minor child and an American citizen, she's my responsibility at the moment," Kelly said. "She insists she has no friends in the village—no one but you, that is. And she wants to stay with you until I locate her father and find out what he wants me to do. I thought of asking the doctor to give her a shot, and then taking her home with me. But that might be a mistaken kindness. I don't know how wise it would be to force her to do something she doesn't want to do at this particular time."

"Well, half the rooms on this floor are empty, including the one next to mine."

"You'd let her stay with you?"

"Of course," Malcolm said.

"It will probably be only for one night," Kelly said, with obvious relief. "By tomorrow I'll be in touch with her father, and we can make plans to send her home."

"I'll talk to the landlady," Malcolm said, pulling off his robe. "You go tell Jenny to get herself packed."

"She's packed and waiting for you," Kelly said with a hopeless sigh. "I hope this is the best thing for her. And may I say officially, Mr. Malcolm, that I'm very grateful to you."

Malcolm and Kelly walked up the dark street to the *pensione* where Coralee Davis had terminated her visit to Spain and the world. Don Fernando stood in the hallway listening to a tearful old woman in a black dress, who rocked rhythmically from side to side as she poured out her account in a voice that trembled with compassion and excitement and self-importance. Don Fernando wrote wearily in a small note-book; his manner was harassed and despairing, as if this tragedy had been specifically designed by fate to destroy his sleep and add to his already intolerable burdens.

In the lobby joining the hall, Jenny Davis sat in an over-stuffed chair, with her hands clasped in her lap and a small straw suitcase on the floor beside her feet. She wore black patent-leather slippers, white ankle socks, and a camel's hair coat with shiny white buttons. The lamp above her was unshaded and the strong harsh light made her blonde hair look yellow, and drew vivid shadows on the planes of her small pale face. When Malcolm came into the lobby, she jumped up and ran to him.

"Can't I stay with you?" she said nervously. "I told Mr. Kelly I didn't even know anyone else."

Malcolm held her close to him. "It's all been arranged, Jenny."

Señora Ramoz and her daughter, Maria, were waiting for Malcolm and Jenny. In the room adjoining Malcolm's, the bed was turned down, the lights were glowing, and from somewhere a ragged doll and a bowl of fresh cherries had been appropriated for the dresser.

The news of the tragedy had already swept through the village. Lights gleamed behind shuttered windows, old women tolled their beads, and the priest had gone to his church to pray for the departed soul. All who heard the story were sorrowful, for this misfortune struck at the two most sensitive chords in their emotional range—the loss of a mother, the anguish of the child.

Señora Ramoz and Maria wept uncontrollably as they helped Jenny undress, and searched through her suitcase for a nightgown. Maria, red-eyed and with heaving shoulders, hung her little dresses neatly in the closet; and her mother placed the ragged doll tenderly on the bed pillow, and as she did so her tears fell and moistened the cloth face of the doll, and then it, too, reflected the gloom and unhappiness of the night.

They put Jenny to bed gently and delicately, as if they feared that even the lightest touch of their compassionate hands might bruise her already unendurably wounded and lacerated flesh. They kissed her on both cheeks, smoothed the wisps of tender hair from her forehead and, at last, with dolorous sighs and anguished expressions, retreated tearfully from the room.

Jenny lay completely still beneath the covers. Malcolm sat on the edge of the bed and took her hand.

"I'll leave my door open," he said. "If you want anything just call. Okay?" When she didn't answer he said, "Do you want to talk about it?"

"Yes, that's why I had to stay with you," she said quietly. "My father will have to take me back now, won't he?"

"Yes, I imagine so."

"He's got to," she said in a tight, stubborn voice. "There's no one else to take care of me now. Except him. I had to say that to somebody. I wanted to hear my voice saying it." She looked up at him and he saw a look of speculation in her eyes. "Do you suppose Mommy knew that?"

"It's hard to say."

"She cried ever since Paco got killed. She just stayed in bed and cried. She always told me never to get her pills for her if she'd been to a party. But this was different. It wasn't late, I mean. Sometimes when it was late she'd ask me for her pills, but I wouldn't get them because she'd told me never to. If she was out late and having lots of fun, she told me she couldn't remember how many pills to take. But this was different. It wasn't dangerous."

Her voice was soft and drowsy. She was very nearly asleep, he saw; her eyes were beginning to close slowly, and her eyelashes cast shadows like dark, delicate brush marks against her white cheeks.

"It was different, because it wasn't late," she said, sighing deeply. "She was crying about Paco, and she had to drink some brandy because of her cold. And so I got them for her. It was early, just after dinner, and she hadn't been to a party or anything."

"Yes. that was different," Malcolm said slowly.

"I had to tell you that, too. And about going back to my father."

"We can talk about it tomorrow. Go to sleep now."

"It doesn't matter, does it? That's what you said. Whether it was different or not, it doesn't matter."

"Please go to sleep."

She turned on her side, and put a thin, pale arm gently about the little doll. "Can you leave my light on?" she asked him, but in such a thick, murmuring voice that he had to lean forward to catch the words.

"Yes, of course. Good-night."

She didn't answer him. He listened a moment to the soft steady rhythm of her breathing, and then stood and walked quietly from the room.

In the corridor, he stopped and leaned against the wall. Something seemed to have shifted inside him, but so abruptly and disturbingly that for an instant he had almost lost his balance.

He frowned faintly. It was a curious sensation, a ridiculous one really, for it made him feel vulnerable. He smiled then, and the ridiculous feeling was gone.

He was still smiling as he entered his dark room.

As he reached for the light beside his bed, Malcolm merged with the darkness of the room. He hadn't heard the step behind him, or a soft hissing noise that split the air with a sound like tearing silk.

There was no pain, only the total merger with darkness.

16

ZARREN said, "I'm taking you to Señor Quesada."

They were driving up a winding road above Málaga. The lights of the city were far below them, and beyond that cluster of brightness was the glitter of the fishing boats against the sky.

"I have no objection," Malcolm said. There was a lump the size of a pigeon's egg at the back of his head. He smiled at Zarren's gloomy profile. "Why did you assume I would?"

"There was no point talking about it. The child next to

your room might have heard. I thought it best to bring you along without discussion."

Malcolm was still smiling, "A lack of imagination is the mother of melodrama," he said. "And who is Señor Quesada?"

"I imagine he will tell you."

The road circled the mountain like the grooves of a corkscrew, and the car's motor labored and whined in the thinning air.

"Is Señor Quesada the one I'm going to kill?"

"No."

After a dozen more swaying revolutions about the narrowing mountain, they came to a clearing where dim yellow postern lamps marked the entrance to a villa. In their faint glow, Malcolm saw stately iron gates and white stone walls stretching away into the darkness.

Zarren turned the car around with a series of inexpert lunges, and snapped off the motor. In the silence, Malcolm could hear the incredibly sweet song of nightingales on the mountain slopes below them; the sound was dizzying in its limpid, swooning perfection.

The scent of jasmine on the cool air was cloyingly appropriate, and Malcolm had the whimsical notion that they had stumbled on a haven of elves and fairies. He imagined them tiptoeing through forests of glucose and treacle to worship at a twinkling shrine of Hans Christian Andersen.

"Get out and go to the gate," Zarren said. "Someone will take you to Señor Quesada."

"You're not coming?"

"No."

"I feel you may be missing something," Malcolm said. He glanced at Zarren's heavy, somber face. "Perhaps a rush of little feet, the sweet tinkle of childish laughter—who knows? Maybe somebody's baking a pie in Peter's Pan."

Zarren looked at him, and the faint light from the dashboard touched the cold sullen anger in his eyes. "Listen to me," he said, slowly and heavily. "I told you why I need money. To bring my brother out of Warsaw. He will die if I don't help him. You laughed at me. You said I was a fool." Zarren took a cigarette lighter from his pocket, and when he spun the wheel against the flint, a flame spurted up and drove the darkness away from his face. "Look at me," Zarren said. "You must kill someone or there is no money. If you don't do it, I will kill you. Look at my eyes when I say it. I will kill you. I want you to believe that."

Zarren was serious, Malcolm knew. There was no doubt of it. Conviction was stamped on his broad heavy face; it glittered in his eyes; vibrated from the tips of his blond mustache. Yes, he was a fine example of seriousness.

"I believe you," Malcolm said smiling. "Tell me, do you remember the dilemma of the good Jews of Shirley, Long Island, when they decided to build a synagogue? They realized they'd have to call it Shirley Temple."

"You don't mind dying," Zarren said slowly. "You think it's funny?"

"I'm not quite sure," Malcolm said. "I was only trying to cheer you up."

Zarren held the lighter closer to Malcolm's face, and stared into his eyes across the tiny, spurting flame. "Listen," Zarren said. "I will kill you so that dying will be a great relief. Do you understand?"

"I can only repeat, a lack of imagination is the mother of melodrama," Malcolm said wearily. "You're a serious man, Zarren, but you're a fool. And seriousness in a fool is like a raw egg in a glass of champagne—it just won't do. I'm serious too, but I'm not a fool."

Malcolm smiled and placed the palm of his hand just above the flickering flame of the lighter. There was pain, of course, that surprised him somewhat, for he hadn't actually expected it. But he realized that he must have been too optimistic or too unrealistic, and perhaps both; for he hadn't suspended his physical reactions and reflexes—juices still flowed through his body, his heart went pumping on, his stomach needed food, his nerve ends writhed spasmodically at the touch of painful external stimuli, and these things proved that he was still a live and functioning animal. But he did feel curiously objective about the sensation in the palm of his hand; he felt as if he were watching it rather than experiencing it.

He closed his hand and extinguished the flame.

In the darkness he heard Zarren's heavy breathing, as slow and resigned as that of a wounded animal.

"Leave your brother in Warsaw," Malcolm said. "Do him that favor. Then he'll live forever hating you."

Malcolm got out of the car and walked over uneven ground to the tall iron gates. In the light of the postern lamps he saw a man behind the bars, a stocky figure who wore a broad leather belt drawn diagonally across a gray twill jacket. There was a shotgun in the crook of the man's arm. He unlocked the gate, but the sound of iron grating on iron was lost in the sudden acceleration of Zarren's car. Malcolm turned and watched the headlights sweeping down the curving road at what seemed to him reckless speed.

"Please come with me," the guard said.

Malcolm followed him along a flagstone path which circled through dark, fragrant gardens. Ahead of them lights appeared above the massive doorway of a white villa. The smooth stone steps leading to the doors were flanked by crouching leopards carved from pale green marble.

The doors were opened by a smiling maid in a black uniform. Malcolm accompanied her down a broad corridor lined with massive chests and cabinets, and lighted at regular intervals by lamps in heavy brass mountings. At the end of the corridor the maid knocked softly on a closed door. Then she opened it, smiled at Malcolm, and stepped aside.

He smiled at her and walked into the room.

There was a fragrant blend of coffee and tobacco and wood smoke in the air. The room was like a reception hall in the embassy of a wealthy country; it was so long that Malcolm noticed the walls of books, the softly glowing rugs, and the paintings that common sense told him weren't originals (although his instinct told him they were) before he noticed the man who sat facing him from a table in front of the fireplace.

The fireplace was at the opposite end of the room and Malcolm didn't recognize the man from that distance.

"Señor Quesada?"

"Yes. I'm pleased you could come. Would you join me for breakfast?"

Malcolm recognized him then, as he approached the table, which was covered with a stiff, white cloth, and laid with two place settings. There was a silver coffee pot on an electric warmer plate, and this was circled by silver bowls containing honey and marmalade, toast and *croissants*.

"It's quite early for breakfast, I realize," Señor Quesada said. "I hope you have some appetite."

"And your bulls? They're well?"

"As a rule, I have only coffee and a roll, with just some honey or marmalade. But if you would like some bacon and eggs, or ham and eggs—something heartier—it will be no trouble at all."

"I'll just have coffee," Malcolm said, and sat down facing the tall, silver-haired man he had met in Domingo's cave the night that Paco's body and soul had been marked for terminal collection.

"You said you were a foreman on a bull ranch. Why?"

"It's not important, I assure you. I am Señor Quesada now, and that isn't important either, I'm afraid." He filled Malcolm's cup. "I wish you would try one of these *croissants*. They're warm, and my cook prides himself on them."

Señor Quesada wore a dark gray suit, a white shirt and tie and a light gray vest on which a gold watch chain glittered dully. He looked calm and cheerful and confident, with a suggestion of peasant shrewdness in his long, brown face and peasant strength in his clean, quiet hands. The firelight gleamed on his beautiful white hair, and made a pattern of shadows in the network of wrinkles at the corners of his eyes. At his elbow were papers and notebooks, and a thick leather wallet secured with a gold clasp. He gestured to them and smiled apologetically.

"I am leaving shortly, which explains my early breakfast and this last minute press of work. But I don't enjoy riding to the airport on an empty stomach. Please help yourself, Mr. Malcolm."

The rolls were warm, the honey was delicious, the coffee was strong and hot. Everything in the room reflected a subtle flavor of quality and permanence. The logs in the fireplace were slim and long, the color of old silver, and they burned with a gentle consistent flame, without so much as a crack or a pop or a wisp of smoke. They must have been aged like wine, Malcolm thought, and trucked down from the north. Or flown in, more likely. The pictures were astonishing. They had no business in anybody's home. It was like walking into a business office and finding the Kohinoor diamond in use as a paper weight. These twisted, royal faces and elongated saints weren't made for private contemplation. Not any more. Not in this year of grace. They were more than pictures now, he thought; they were resplendent markers on old majestic roads of art and history, and they should be entombed in large gray museums, where school children could be made to look at them and where experts could fight over them to their hearts' content.

Malcolm nodded at one particular painting, embracing with this casual gesture about a million dollars worth of canvas and oil.

"I have the ridiculous feeling that's genuine," he said.

Señor Quesada smiled. "Oh yes, it's real enough." He pointed toward a row of portraits glowing under gallery lights. "Those were commissioned by my family, originally. The El Greco, which you seem to appreciate, was a gift for one thing or another. By today's values they are impressive. But they were painted for a fraction of that, remember. It's one advantage of being the last shoot from a very old family tree.

"It's almost as if one owned a time machine and could go back a few hundred years and invest thousands with the Rothschilds at six or eight per cent." Señor Quesada laughed ruefully. "Just think of it! To return to the present and collect a fortune, which had grown and swollen with each tick of the clock, with every turn of the seasons, multiplying itself as each year, each decade, each century passed into history."

Señor Quesada sighed philosophically and began to butter a roll.

"After you've killed this person for Domingo, what are your plans?" He smiled pleasantly at Malcolm. "Providing you get away with it, as they say in your country. What do you intend to do then?"

"I don't know."

Señor Quesada considered this reply as he carefully spread a layer of honey over his buttered roll.

"You don't know? Or you don't care?"

"Both, I imagine," Malcolm said.

"Can you remember four numbers?"

"I think so."

Señor Quesada spoke in Spanish for the first time. *"Ocho. Quatro. Cinco. Seis."*

Malcolm repeated them in English. "Eight, four, five, six."

"Keep that number in mind when you've fulfilled your obligation to Domingo. It's the telephone number of my office in Lausanne. You may call there any time of the day or night, it doesn't matter. I would like to talk with you when you are free."

"I'm free now," Malcolm said smiling.

"I understand, but I prefer to wait. You possess an unusual talent, which you are exercising for Domingo for a very reasonable price. A glass of brandy, wasn't it?"

"Cheap brandy," Malcolm said. He was still smiling at Señor Quesada. Everything seemed suddenly so clear to him now that he nearly blinked his eyes in surprise; it was the way he had felt when he had first looked at the village after making his bargain with Domingo—all details in sharp focus, commonplace objects significantly refined, the total effect being that of having suddenly reached a fresh and harmonious definition of terms with the physical world.

"But you didn't trust Domingo's estimate of my unusual talent," he said.

"Of course not. He offered me the choice of an assassin without a pedigree, if you will. I was interested in the guns Clarke had discovered, but when I learned that bringing them into Spain depended on you. . . ." Señor Quesada smiled apologetically. "A paid killer is one thing. But Domingo's confidence in you seemed based on very flimsy evidence. But he was insistent. He pleaded with me. His conviction seemed unhealthy and unreasonable, but it was so strong that I agreed to be present at the test he arranged with Paco. I watched you carefully that night. You did not know the gun wasn't loaded. And when I saw your finger tighten on the trigger, and studied the look in your eye, I knew that Domingo's confidence had not been misplaced."

Malcolm sipped his coffee and tried with difficulty to keep a straight face. Something very funny had occurred to him, and he could hear laughter like bright distant thunder exploding inside him.

"Domingo is working for you then," he said, choosing a tranquilizing topic in the hope that it would deaden or deflect his comical reflections.

"He is my agent, yes."

"And why do you want to smuggle guns into Spain? To seize power? To overthrow the government?"

"That's a headache only a fool would choose for himself," Señor Quesada said with a dry smile. "I'd like to know if the plan will work, for one thing. It's only an experiment. Domingo is a pathetic creature. So are the men working with him. They are risking their lives for very small amounts of money. But I've agreed to buy the guns, providing they are safely brought into Spain."

"And what are you going to do with them?"

"I will let them be discovered by the police."

"That makes sense."

Señor Quesada laughed cheerfully. "Indeed it does, although I suspect you were being sarcastic." He put his elbows on the table, laced his fingers together, and regarded Malcolm with an indulgent smile. "The priests use a simple argument to convince children of the existence of God. It goes like this: if you see a chair, you must believe in a carpenter. The chair couldn't saw itself into proper lengths, and hammer itself together, of course. And so when you see a tree, you must believe in the existence of a God. For the tree, too, must have a maker. I am wondering if this simple reasoning will be employed when a cache of rifles is discovered in some appropriately remote and sinister hiding place. Will it be anxiously assumed that there is a rebel force trained and ready to use these guns?"

"Is there such a force?"

Señor Quesada shrugged casually. "I have no idea. But I may find out. Accurate information is always valuable. If Spain joins the Common Market of Europe, and Belgium is affronted by this, if France and America continue to bicker over whose hands are worthy to push certain buttons in the event of war with Russia—then everything I can learn of what lines the Bishop of Seville will delete from his next sermon, or of the mood of the miners in Navarre, may help me to judge what may develop in more significant areas. As I told you the guns are an experiment. I am also experimenting with certain notions in South Africa, and various others in Europe. But we can talk of these things later. Do you remember the number in Lausanne?"

"Eight, four, five, six."

"Good. I want you to call me."

"One thing puzzles me," Malcolm said.

"Yes?"

"You're going to considerable bother and expense in this matter," Malcolm said. "And further bother and expense, I presume, to bribe some maid to bring you the contents of a bishop's wastebasket and so forth. But supposing you draw the wrong conclusions from these facts?"

"That wouldn't matter."

"And if you draw the correct conclusions? What then?"

Señor Quesada looked at him oddly. There was definite disappointment in his expression. "I thought you understood me," he said. "In fact, I was quite sure of it."

The old man's eyes were steady and penetrating, and Malcolm felt again the thrill of recognition as he looked into their depths.

"Either way it doesn't matter? Is that it?"

"Yes, of course."

"How long have you believed this?"

Señor Quesada looked thoughtful. "I think I was born with that conviction. To know, as you and I know, that things are meaningless, is probably a form of insanity. It stems from an ability or need to alter reality. To live comfortably with illogical distortions requires a curious attitude toward life. Mine was bred into me, by ancestors who complacently taught the gentle love of Jesus Christ with racks and red-hot pincers. Their minds didn't crack with the strain of holding such opposed notions in sweet accord. But that's a primitive example. You'll find all sorts of people who can make such accommodations in the light of self-interest. But to cheerfully contemplate and acknowledge the unreality of reality is a much more subtle accomplishment."

"Are there many like us—outside of institutions, that is?"

"Probably more than you would imagine."

Malcolm found his bottled-up laughter becoming painful; it reminded him of an exquisite but heroically contained hysteria he had once experienced—along with the rest of the class—when a Latin instructor had translated the sentence, "Galba was stung on his thigh," as "Galba was stung on his thing."

He rubbed his lips to hide a smile. "These guns Clarke came across—they were in Algeria?"

"Yes, they were stored somewhere near Colomb-Bechar."

"German rifles, of course."

"Of course," Señor Quesada said, frowning faintly. "But how did you know that?"

"I overheard some talk."

"I see. Yes, they're Model 41's, a gas-operated rifle which the Germans experimented with in World War II. Many of them were abandoned during the African campaigns. Clarke found a good supply, four-hundred and fifty-odd, I believe. They'll be transported from Colomb-Bechar to Sidi-bel-Abbès, and then on to the port of Ceuta." Señor Quesada tilted his head slightly and regarded Malcolm with a perplexed smile. "Would you mind telling me why you find all this so amusing?"

"I'm sorry, I can't help it," he said. The convolutions of fact and fancy created such delicious nonsense before his eyes that he couldn't check his laughter any longer; he put his head back and it flowed from him in breathless convulsions.

Señor Quesada's eyebrows rose in polite amazement.

"It's the plan," Malcolm said at last. He wiped a tear from his eyes. "Forgive me, but the last part is just too much." He knew that he was right, of course; he knew that his wild guess would match the designs so relentlessly forged by Domingo and his cohorts. "To bring the rifles in with fishing nets," he said. "It's so simple I find it terribly funny."

Now Señor Quesada was smiling too, and there was a suggestion of complacence in the graceful curve of his lips. "That was my idea," he said.

This nearly set Malcolm off again. But he checked himself with an effort. "It's fabulous," he said.

Señor Quesada seemed both pleased and embarrassed to accept credit for this final bit of ingenuity. "Yes, it's clever," he said, with a modest and deprecating smile. "Fifteen boats can bring the rifles in quite easily. The fishermen have been told the crates contain whiskey. They will never know otherwise. The crates will be trucked away from the beach in a matter of minutes." He picked up the thick leather wallet, and unsnapped the gold clasp.

"You remember my number in Lausanne?"

"Yes, of course."

Señor Quesada opened the wallet and its gold-bound corners flashed brightly as he removed a thick white envelope and placed it in front of Malcolm. "This will remind you to get in touch with me," he said. "Call it a down payment for future services, if you like."

"Thank you," Malcolm said, and put the envelope in the inside pocket of his jacket.

"My car is waiting to take you to the village," Señor Quesada said as he rose to his feet. "Let me wish you good luck. I'll be interested to know how things work out. Unfortunately, I'll be a long way from here then, but I'll be advised of the outcome."

"I have a question I'd like to ask you," Malcolm said, as they walked toward the door.

"And that is?"

"Do you read detective stories?"

Señor Quesada smiled and shook his head. "I find them a bore."

"I figured you would," Malcolm said.

They shook hands formally in the light falling through the great double doors of the villa. Their smiles were rather alike then, amused and intimate, as they said good-bye to one another between the figures of the crouching green leopards.

Then Malcolm walked down the winding patch through the gardens to where a long black car waited for him in the glow of the postern lamps.

He was still smiling; and he felt sure that this smile, this knowledge, was an armor to last him all his life.

17

DOMINGO'S bar was closed for the night, but a light still burned above the poker table, where Domingo sat with Zarren and the Spaniard, Jorge. The cards were idle, the chips stacked away in a wooden rack. The men were not talking. There was a smell of tobacco and sour wine on the air, and the cold winds that blew heavily against the windows spread a damp, uncomfortable chill through the room.

The faintest sounds caught and held their attention; they turned their eyes quickly and restlessly to the fall of ashes in the black stove, to the drip of water from a faucet, or the creak of roof timbers in the high winds.

Finally Domingo pulled a watch from his vest pocket and stared at it with a frown. Then he said, "It's late."

Zarren touched a match to a black cigarette and said nothing.

"Will you use the American?" Jorge said to Domingo.

The Frenchman fingered the lead bullet attached to his watch chain, and the frown deepened on his face. "I don't know."

Jorge rested his elbows on the table and leaned forward to smile at Domingo. "He won't do it. I'm sure of that."

Domingo shrugged and drummed his fingers on the table top. Lines of tension were drawn deeply into his face; in spite of the vast and seemingly imperturbable bulk of his body, there was something about him which suggested a wire drawn just short of its breaking point.

Jorge turned his smile to Zarren. "You think the American will do it? You think his promise means anything?"

Zarren looked sadly at the lighter he still held in his hand. "Yes, he will do it."

"No, you're wrong," Jorge said. "Once I put my foot against his backside, and kicked him into the gutter. I could do it again now. He hasn't changed, he's the same man."

"He took your woman," Domingo said, watching him with

a faint smile. "Is that why you bluster while he's not here?"

"She was not my woman."

Domingo laughed. "That was her choice. But you wanted her, didn't you? You liked her, eh?"

"I do not talk of such things," Jorge said with dignity. "What a man feels for a woman, or doesn't feel for her, is nothing to discuss in bars with other men."

"Here we talk about anything I want," Domingo said slowly, and now the anger smouldering inside him was nakedly and dangerously evident in his flushed face and small, hot eyes. "You hear me? I decide what we talk about. Answer me—you like Tani, eh?"

Jorge was pale. "She can be pleasant," he said carefully. "She had moods which are agreeable. Yes, I like her."

Zarren let out his breath slowly.

Domingo was still staring at Jorge. "I'm giving you one night's work which pays more than two years in a fishing boat. Don't tell me what you like to talk about."

Zarren took out his watch. "The trucks are waiting," he said.

"And the fishermen are waiting," Domingo said angrily "We are waiting, everything waits for Clarke, and he may be drunk or sick or dead."

Zarren collected the cards and looked at them gloomily. "Shall we play?"

Jorge reached for the chips, but Domingo shook his head and the Spaniard shrugged and lit a cigarette.

The silence was disturbed minutes later by the sound of a laboring engine. Domingo cocked his head to the noise, and then stood quickly and walked to the window. He pulled the curtain aside and saw, on the road from Cartama, two slender beams of light probing into the darkness like the feelers of a bug.

He smiled with relief and let the curtain fall back into place. Glancing once more at his watch. he unlocked the front door.

Clarke came into the bar with rapid strides; he moved in a jerky, disjointed manner, as if all the motors inside him were running at varying and erratic speeds. "Get me a bloody drink," he said, as he pulled off his cap and sank into a chair at the poker table. His face was so pale and his voice was so thin and tight with tension that Domingo snapped his fingers angrily at Jorge.

"Bring him some brandy, quick!"

Clarke sighed wearily and ran a hand over his gray, sweat-streaked face. "I haven't slept since I left here," he said in a bitter, petulant voice.

"You'll have plenty of time to sleep," Domingo said. "What's the matter?"

Jorge carried a full tumbler of brandy to the table, and Clarke drank it down in slow, deliberate gulps. The liquor brought points of color into his cheeks, and a warm, wet shine to his eyes. He coughed convulsively for an instant, and then looked up and said to Domingo, "The rifles put to sea on schedule. They'll be a mile off the coast by dawn."

Domingo looked at him in bewilderment. "It's all right then. The trucks and fishing boats are waiting. What's the matter with you?"

"Just this: a local copper in Ceuta had an exact description of the rifles. Knew where they were coming from, knew where they were going." Clarke drew a deep, unsteady breath. "That's what's wrong. Don Fernando tipped him off—he knows every bloody move we've made."

Domingo stared at Zarren and Jorge, and the silence became thick and oppressive. "Who told him?" he said, in a thick, straining voice.

"No need to look at them," Clarke said. "The copper in Ceuta was cooperative after a bit. Don Fernando got his leads from Tani."

Domingo sat down heavily at the poker table. He looked like a nervous Buddha, with sweat shining on his forehead, and a muscle jerking unevenly beside his left eye. "All right, go and bring her here," he said at last to Jorge. He pulled out his watch and studied it anxiously. "There still may be time."

Jorge started toward the door, but Domingo stopped him with a snap of his fingers. "She has a rubber bathing cap. Bring that, too."

"A bathing cap?" Jorge said stupidly. "What for?"

"You'll see," Domingo said.

Señor Quesada's car dropped Malcolm at his *pensione* early in the morning. It was quite cold. A wind was rising and there was no hint as yet of daylight on the horizon. The whole world seemed to be sleeping, Malcolm thought. as he looked up and down the silent street.

He felt alert and wide awake after his encounter with Señor Quesada, and he knew there was no point in trying to sleep now, so he turned and walked down the street to the tiny, irregular plaza which spread out from the stone steps of the church.

Since the doors stood open and the night was cold, Malcolm went inside and sat down in a back pew.

Candles glowed on the altar alongside the tabernacle, and vigil lights burned with spurting red flames in a brass rack before the communion rail. Malcolm saw the white head of the old priest through the gloom; his body was a thin black cylinder at the *prie-dieu* beside the stairs which spiralled to the pulpit.

The church was small and warm and on the air was an ancient fragrance—more something remembered than experienced—of flowers and incense and cold marble.

The money Señor Quesada had given him was a comfortable weight in his jacket. Twenty-five hundred dollars in pesetas and Swiss francs pressed lightly but warmly against the steady beat of his heart, and Malcolm thought of the money and tried to measure its potential in terms of his own future existence.

He could go away tonight if he wanted to. And take Tani with him. They could go to Paris. She seemed to like that city. Paris could be pleasant and snug in the winter. He knew a street near St. Germain des Prés where an old woman sold violets on the corner all winter long. They could find an apartment and be comfortable until the days became warm and all the city glowed with the radiance of spring. Very nice, he thought. Paris in the spring was Tani. Or they could go to Morocco. To the exquisite city of Marrakesh, and live in a hotel with a veiw of gardens and palm trees. In the morning they would share breakfast with the song birds on the terrace. Very pleasant, too, he thought. To feed song birds with Tani in the warm sunshine of Marrakesh.

He smiled and watched the curling tips of the candles as they cast shifting lights through the gloom of the church.

These thoughts of his were only pleasant traps, he knew, alluring cages. The doors stood temptingly open for anyone lonely enough or unwitting enough to dream of realizing such kinds of happiness.

Malcolm stood and walked to the wooden collection box which hung on the wall beside the holy water font. He took Señor Quesada's money from his pocket, and methodically began stuffing it through the slot cut into the top of the box. The slot was quite narrow; it had been designed for coins, not these large crisp banknotes, and he was forced to feed the money through it piece by piece, folding the bills so that they slid comfortably down the small throat of the box.

He heard a soft footstep behind him and turned to find the old priest watching him with alarm.

"What are you doing here?"

"I'm making a contribution to the poor of the village."

The priest came forward slowly, and stared at the banknotes with an expression blended of hope and suspicion, of eagerness and fear. "It is a fortune," he said. "Is it stolen? Is it evil?"

"You'll give it to good people. How can it be evil?"

At last he was through. All the money was gone. He smiled a good-bye to the priest and went outside.

The money had been a heavy burden, he realized; now he felt light and free once more, and he knew that he could go to bed and fall asleep with no trouble at all. . . .

Zarren barred the heavy wooden door of the cave which had been hollowed from the mountain behind Domingo's bar.

Clarke and Jorge bound Tani to a chair beneath the naked electric bulb that hung on a cord from the ceiling.

Domingo stood in front of her and slapped a bright red bathing cap softly and rhythmically against the palm of his hand. "We must know what you told the policeman," he said.

"But I told him nothing," she said frantically.

There was no sound in the cold damp cave except her quick, shallow breathing, and the slow trickle of water down the stone walls. She had bitten Clarke's hand and thrust a knee into Jorge's groin as they struggled with her, but now she was helpless and vulnerable, her arms bound behind her and her ankles tied back against the heavy crossbars which braced the legs of the chair. The overhead light beat directly down on her shining black hair, but its glare was icy, without warmth or mercy. She wore only a shirt, a pair of slacks and slippers, and already the cold and damp of the cave were cutting into her like knives. As she stared up at the faces looming above her in the shadows, a shiver of fear ran along her bare arms and legs. Their eyes were like stones, their mouths like bitter traps.

She smiled piteously. "Someone has told you lies about me. Why should I want to cause trouble for you?"

"I don't care why you did it," Domingo said, patiently and earnestly. "But I must know what you told him."

"You're a fool," she said, She tried to sound angry and contemptuous. "I didn't tell him anything."

"I'll give you sixty seconds to think of another answer," Domingo said. "Sixty seconds without air," he added and snapped the rubber bathing cag over her face so deftly and swiftly that her attempts to evade it were hopeless; even before she could flinch from his hands, the cap was in place, fitted snugly from beneath her chin to the crown of her dark head, hermetically sealing off the air from her face.

Domingo turned his back on her and took out his watch. After an interval, he said. "Ten seconds, Tani. Only ten seconds. You still have lots of time to think of another answer."

Zarren looked away and rubbed his hands together nervously. He drew a slow, deep breath and held it.

"Twenty seconds," Domingo said quietly.

Jorge's forehead was blistered with tiny beads of sweat. He stared at the ceiling and began to count silently; his lips looked as if they were moving in prayer.

Only Clarke watched Tani. He sucked deeply and gratefully on his cigarette, and then put his bleeding hand to his mouth and licked the place where she had bitten him with quick thrusts of his tongue.

"Forty seconds," Domingo said, and Zarren released the air from his lungs with an explosive gasp.

The bright red bathing cap was molded against Tani's face like a death mask; every crease and wrinkle had been flattened out by the straining suction of her lungs.

"I have counted to sixty," Jorge cried to Domingo. "Now it's past sixty."

"By my watch, it is only fifty," Domingo said.

Tani's body arched rhythmically and powerfully against the ropes binding her into the chair; it was a mechanical spasmodic response, as if strong currents of electricity were being shot down her spine at methodical intervals.

"Now it is sixty," Domingo said. He replaced the watch in his vest pocket and slowly removed the bathing cap from Tani's face. "I hope you've had enough time to think of a better answer."

The sound of her harsh, frantic breathing nearly drowned out his words. Blood trickled from her nostrils, and her eyes bulged so that the tears glittering in them looked as if they had been squeezed from her pale face by a vise.

"Now let's have the truth," Domingo said. "You told the policeman about the guns?"

"Yes," she said weakly.

"Tell me everything."

"I told him about the German rifles in Algeria." Tani's head felt so curiously light and empty that it was very simple to remember all the details. "They were Model 41's, experimental rifles. You planned to bring them into Spain. That's all I knew. That's all I told Don Fernando."

"Did you know how we were bringing them into Spain?"

"Yes."

"And you told him that?"

"Yes."

Domingo sighed heavily. "That's very bad."

Zarren looked at him. "You must use him now. There's no other way."

"It's a waste," Domingo said sadly. "I wanted to save him for something else." He shrugged his massive shoulders, as if he was trying to unburden himself of heavy regrets and disappointments. Then he looked thoughtfully at Tani. "Where did you learn this? Who told you about the guns?"

"One night an old man came to see me. He was a Dutchman, I think." Tani's head was so blessedly clear and empty, that she could imagine him in vivid detail; it was as if her mind were an empty stage, and an old man had suddenly stepped down to the footlights. "He was very tall, but he stooped when he walked so he didn't look as tall as he really was. His hair was thick and white, and he wore glasses without any rims. He told me he was a mate on a ship in Tangier. On the back of his left hand there was a tattoo mark, a red dagger in a blue circle."

"And he told you all about the German rifles?"

She nodded quickly. "Yes, I swear it."

"How did he know about them?"

"He heard some people talking about them. Some men. In a bar."

"Where?"

"In Tangier." She began to weep softly. "Please let me go. I didn't believe him. I thought he was just making up a story. If I'd believed him, I would never have gone to Don Fernando. But I didn't know the story was true. I thought it was a joke."

"This was a very unusual looking man," Domingo said quietly. "A Dutchman with white hair and tattooed hands and glasses without rims. It's strange I never saw him. Did you, Zarren?"

"No."

"Clarke?"

"No."

"Jorge? Did you see him?"

"No."

"He was only here one night," Tani said helplessly.

"I am going to give you some more time to think," Domingo said.

She looked into his eyes, and realized what she must do; for she was too weak and too frightened to endure anything else. Tani thought of Malcolm who had given her the illusion of love, and then, as Domingo began to slip the cap over her face again, she quietly and deliberately released all the air from her lungs.

This time not even Clarke could watch.

There was no sound in the room but the drip of water from the walls, the steady tick of Domingo's watch, and one other sound, a faint, almost pleasant sound, like that of sails pulling slowly against their rigging, and this came from the ropes twisting against the pressure of Tani's straining wrists and ankles.

18

CLARKE came to Malcolm's room at four in the morning.

"Now you're going to pay for that bloody drink," he said. "Get into your clothes."

He looked even more wretched than usual, Malcolm thought; under a peaked cap the Englishman's small face was pinched and white, and the cigarette in his mouth shook with the tremor of his lips.

"All right," Malcolm said, and began to dress.

Clarke took an automatic with black handgrips from the pocket of his raincoat and removed the magazine from it. Then he gave the gun to Malcolm.

"You're ready?"

"Yes."

Clarke stared into his eyes. Then he gave him the loaded magazine. "Slip that in, and you're in business. It throws a bit high and left, but don't let it worry you. You'll be just across the desk from him."

"The desk?"

"Yes, it's the policeman, Don Fernando."

"Will he be at his office now?"

"Some kind but anonymous stranger called him at his home to tell him the sad news of what happened to his friend in Ceuta." Clarke took the cigarette from his mouth and dropped it on the floor. "It seems his friend got stuck with a knife and thrown into the harbor. Don Fernando's at his office waiting for all the details—which the kind stranger promised to come and tell him. So you just walk in and do your job."

"I see," Malcolm said, and slipped on his jacket.

Clarke watched him with bitter eyes. "It's just a piece of cake, eh? A milk run, is that it?"

"You're nervous," Malcolm said. "Why not just shut up and let me get on with it?"

"You enjoy playing the hero, eh? Well, you almost missed your chance." He stared at Malcolm with the trace of a smile touching his gray lips. "Like Domingo says, it's kind of a waste. It isn't often you find a zombie ready to pull a trigger for you. We planned for you to kill the policeman all along, then bring in the guns during what you could call the ensuing flap. But for a while it looked like we didn't need to. Everything was so cozy and quiet we might have dragged the bloody things ashore at high noon. But now that honeymoon's over. The guns are standing off the coast a mile north of here, and we've got to kill the policeman before they come in. Because Tani told him what we're up to."

Malcolm turned and stared at him. "How do you know that?"

"Because she admitted it. With a bit of persuasion, of course. Little red bathing cap did the job. Simple trick. Only a fool wouldn't trade information for a lungful of air after a bit." Clarke watched Malcolm closely. "I've seen that electrical gadget used on prisoners in Algeria," he said. "Clamp it on a chap's love muscle, run the current up and down a few times, and you'd get what you wanted from him on the double quick. But the bathing cap's almost as good, and not near the bother." He smiled suddenly. "You don't like this, eh? I can see it in your face."

Malcolm spoke with an effort. "Where is she?"

"Funny thing," Clarke said, still smiling with satisfaction at Malcolm. "She told us everything but where she got the information. At this stage of the game, it wasn't important. But she acted like it was. She acted like it was worth more than anything else in the world."

"Where is she?" Malcolm said again.

"She's dead," Clarke said coldly and quietly. "Dead and gone, chum. We put her back in her bed. It'll look like a hemorrhage took her while she was sleeping." He snapped his cigarette-stained fingers. "Like that. Good way to go. Quick and neat."

"You killed her?" Malcolm sat down slowly on the edge of the bed. "You killed her?"

Clarke studied him with interest. "It hurts, eh? Something gets through to you, I guess."

"You shouldn't have killed her," Malcolm said, in a soft, empty voice.

"She wouldn't talk. She begged for it. Domingo obliged her."

Malcolm began to laugh. "Because she wouldn't tell who told her about the guns—that's why he killed her?"

"That's more your style, that's better," Clarke said. "Treat it like a joke." Suddenly his lips began to tremble. "But you weren't there. It's destroyed me. All the locks in the world won't help now. But just see you do your job. I've got enough left in me to kill you if you don't."

He pulled open the door and left the room.

Malcolm sat motionless on the bed until Clarke's footsteps faded down the hallway. He was still laughing softly. On the table beside him stood the tiny pink shepherd dog which Tani had given him. For a long time Malcolm sat laughing quietly, and staring at the floor, for he couldn't make himself turn and look at the little dog which had guarded her herd of plastic sheep. But finally he picked it up and stared at it. Then he rose unsteadily and went into the the bathroom. In the mirror above the handbasin he looked at his pale face and staring eyes for a long moment, and then he screamed hoarsely and smashed his reflection to bits with a blow of his fist.

He knelt beside the toilet and tried to vomit up the horror inside him, but he could only choke and gasp until a liquid distilled of shame and revulsion rose to scald his throat like acid. For a long time he knelt beside the toilet, praying for the pain in his head to explode and kill him. . . .

Malcolm walked with long, purposeful strides down the twisting street which led to Don Fernando's office. This must go well, he told himself; he must be calm and authoritative, and above all, quick, for even now there was a vague promise of light on the horizon.

In the right-hand pocket of his raincoat Clarke's automatic hung against his thigh coldly and reassuringly.

Don Fernando sat at his desk, and the light above him pitilessly marked the lines of anxiety in his pale and haggard face.

Malcolm stood facing him with his hands in his pockets. He glanced once at the felt-trimmed windows to gauge the progress of dawn, and then stared down at Don Fernando.

"It wasn't you who called me," Don Fernando said uneasily. "It was a Spaniard."

"I don't know anything about that."

"Can you tell me of Manuel Hernandez? Someone called to tell me he was killed in Ceuta last night."

"I don't know anything about him."

Don Fernando studied the hard, cold lines in his face. and attempted to judge the significance of the queer, staring look of his eyes. Then the policeman smiled with a show of indifference, and settled back comfortably in his chair. He hooked a thumb over his cartridge belt, and let his fingers drift casually to the flap of his holster.

"I've been told you were planning to kill someone for Domingo," he said. "Someone you didn't know." He smiled indulgently, as if the notion were both amusing and ridiculous. "For no reason at all."

"You were misinformed," Malcolm said.

"I'm glad to hear that. Killing people is a serious matter." He was still smiling. "I had half a thought that you might have come here to kill me."

"You were in error," Malcolm said. "But I have something to tell you that isn't. The rifles from Ceuta are arriving here at dawn." What had Clarke said? He couldn't make a mistake now. North—it was north.

"They're to come in a mile south of Cartama," Malcolm said. "I know that's true. I heard it from Domingo."

The policeman's stomach suddenly began to ache with pain. "Until I make an investigation, I must ask you to remain here in my office," he said.

"All right."

The policeman stood and put on his cap. He strode resolutely toward the door, wrapping the dignity of his office about him like a cloak against unseen dangers. But the pain was growing worse, and the slippery pathway he was tread-

142

ing now stretched before him as menacingly as the corridor to a death cell.

Malcolm walked slowly through the damp, heavy sand. Salty wind stung his cheeks, and mingled its flavor with the tears in his eyes. He didn't know he was crying; he wasn't aware of the thick wet sand under his feet, or the waves frothing along the shore. The wind was rising and a streak of thin light, as straight as a ruler, stretched across the horizon.

Malcolm thought he must be in Paris. The light was right for that, and the salt on his lips was like the salt they served with oysters and wedges of lemon in the little stands in Montparnasse. They might find an apartment there, and she would sit quietly before the fireplace waiting for him, sitting so quietly that she could hear the clock ticking in the kitchen.

Along the horizon the flares from the fishing boats stood out vividly against the gray approach of dawn, long irregular strings of light which stretched from Gibraltar to Mälaga and on north to Barcelona, peaceful armadas which had been attacking the Spanish coast every day and every year since long before the birth of Christ. Each boat flew a triangular sail on a single mast, but the sails were hauled in now as the fishermen leaned into their oars to pull the heavy nets back to the beaches.

The shell he thought had been sealed so completely had been cracked into a thousand pieces. To be sure, there was nothing inside now; but Malcolm knew it hadn't always been empty. And he knew the name of the thief who had looted it.

The sand sucked at his shoes and the wind burned the salty tears against his cheeks, like a branding iron. At a curve in the beach he saw two trucks ahead of him in the gray darkness. They were parked at the foot of a narrow road which twisted up to the main highway.

He stopped and drew a deep breath. The wind was higher now, and the surf was pounding like thunder along the shoreline. He took the automatic from his pocket, made sure there was a round in the chamber, and then walked on slowly through the heavy, clinging sand.

Domingo stood with three men at the tailgates of the trucks. In a windbreaker and woollen cap, he loomed enormously in the uncertain light of the false dawn.

Malcolm paid no attention to Clarke and Jorge and Zarren. They were dwarfed by Domingo's great bulk; they were insignificant.

Domingo was staring out at the approaching line of boats. He was smiling, Malcolm realized; he could see the shine of his teeth through the black beard, and the tense, exultant light in his eyes.

He stopped ten feet from him, remembering that Clarke's gun kicked high and to the left.

"Domingo," he said.

The Frenchman turned quickly and frowned at him in surprise and confusion. The light was like the glow of a pearl, and the wind stirred Domingo's beard, and sent the waves charging like white-maned horses at the shore.

"You killed him? You killed the policeman?"

"No," Malcolm said.

"What's the matter with you?"

"Our account's settled," Malcolm said, shouting over the gusting winds. "I killed Paco for you, and the woman he slept with. I killed Tani for you. How many murders do you want for a glass of brandy?"

"You're crazy!" Domingo shouted the words back at him; he walked slowly toward Malcolm, his great thick arms swinging out wide from his body. "You're crazy," he said again. "I killed them. I killed Tani. I didn't want to. She made me."

"Oh, yes, you wanted to kill her," Malcolm said. The wind whipped his hair over his eyes, and tore the words from his mouth, and he realized that he was wasting his breath for Domingo couldn't hear him now; but it seemed important to him, terribly important, to put this conviction into words. "You're a pig, and you can't be happy in anything but a world of swine. She knew that. And you couldn't make her change her mind."

"By God, you're crazy!" Domingo said once more, but anxiously and imploringly now, for Malcolm had raised his gun as he was speaking, and pointed it at his chest.

There was a confused and frightened look on Domingo's face, as if he had just seen a trusted friend turn into a savage enemy before his eyes. "The boats are bringing them in safely," he said, and his tongue curled like a pink snake in his beard when he wet his dry lips. "Don't you understand? It's working as I planned it. Now we can do something bigger, you and I. I need you, I waited for you, don't you believe that? Together we can do something so wonderful the memory will thrill us all our lives. For me, you can do it." He laughed hoarsely and spread his arms in a gesture so wide that it looked as if he were trying to embrace the whole world.

"I cannot be wrong," he cried to Malcolm, but his voice was rising giddily and hysterically now, and he lowered himself to his knees and began to pound on the damp sand with the palm of one enormous hand, as if he were calling on the earth itself to bear witness to the truth of his words. "I'm right, I know it," he shouted frantically. "Listen to me."

Clarke and Zarren and Jorge stood behind him in a semicircle. They studied the Frenchman's kneeling figure with cautious eyes and, with even greater caution, risked occasional glances at the gun in Malcolm's hand.

"You can kill anyone for me," Domingo said desperately, and fumbled for his own gun. "Anyone! The most important man in the world. You can kill him for me."

"Yes, that's what I'm going to do," Malcolm said, and remembering that the automatic kicked high and left, he shot Domingo three times through the heart.

Domingo lay on his back like a beached whale. Malcolm took the watch and chain from his sodden vest, ripped the bullet from it and put it into his pocket. He let the watch and chain fall on the sand as he turned and walked back up the beach.

Zarren stared after him until his figure was lost in the gray gloom of the morning. Then he said wearily, "It's over, finished."

"No, there's a chance," Clarke said.

Jorge stood between them with his hands locked together to stop their trembling.

"There is no chance," Zarren said, still looking down the beach to where Malcolm had merged into the spray from the pounding waves and the trailing mists of dawn. "No chance now. We must send the boats out to deep water and dump the rifles at sea." He nudged Domingo's body with his foot. "We will lash this to a few crates and throw it in, too. The guns will keep him down until the fish finish with him."

Clarke turned and looked with anguished eyes at the line of approaching boats. "They're so close," he cried. "We've got to take a chance."

Zarren shook his head slowly. "We'd be shot or hung within a week if we tried. It's over now. Forget it."

He nodded at Jorge and bent to take hold of Domingo's

arms. Jorge moved quickly to help him. Clarke began to cry. Then he cursed wearily and hopelessly, and reached down for Domingo's legs.

19

NO vigil lights burned in the church for Tani; no lamentations sounded for her in the village. She wasn't buried in the consecrated ground of the cemetery, but in a walled area adjacent to it, which was set aside for anyone careless enough to die in Spain without benefit of clergy. But someone had placed a wooden cross on her grave. and the old priest had gone there to say a prayer, not for Tani since he hadn't known her, but for all children of God unfortunate enough to approach the gates of His Kingdom without the proper visas of sanctifying grace. And someone had left a wreath of artificial flowers beside the marker, a gaudy circle of plastic roses with flecks of gilt paint shining on their petals.

Malcolm went there late one afternoon and looked down at the narrow mound of earth which defined her final resting place. It had rained that morning. Now it was colder and the rain had stopped, but the wind blew drops of water from the trees and these fell in fitful flurries on her grave. The sea beyond was gray and lifeless, and the sky was so low that it seemed to be weighing on the crowns of the trees in the cemetery. Against the base of a broken stone angel, two cats huddled together in an impersonal union against the cold winds.

Malcolm put a fist against his mouth and stared out at the bleak sea. She had been courageous and loyal, he knew; and the fact that he still lived was a cynical, sniggering jest to mock the small dignity of her death.

But above all, was the ghastly inability to ever make amends. . . .

The pattern of soft shadows on her grave altered slightly; the green door of the cemetery creaked open and Don Fernando walked down the stone pathway to join Malcolm at her grave. He was very pale, and his eyes were sorrowful.

"I went a mile south of here last night," he said at last. "I inspected all the boats. There were no rifles."

Malcolm said nothing.

"And where is Domingo now?" the policeman asked him.

"I don't know."

"The others are still here."

"I know that."

Don Fernando was staring anxiously at Tani's grave. "I have been the policeman here for twenty-two years. Sometimes a stone mason falls from a house and is killed. Or a fisherman is lost at sea. The old people died in their beds. And now. . . ." He shrugged helplessley "It's as if God suddenly stopped caring about us."

"Maybe it's enough if just one person stops caring," Malcolm said wearily.

As he turned and walked up the stone pathway, a sudden whipping wind shook the trees, and rain drops fell in a lonely drizzle on all the graves in the cemetery, the new and the old, the tended and neglected, the consecrated and unconsecrated alike; it was as if, he thought bitterly, nature at least was prepared to show she had no interest in such distinctions. He stopped and felt in his pocket for the little pink shepherd dog she had given him. Then he walked back to her grave and put the plastic dog on the wet ground beside the wreath of artificial flowers.

In his room Jenny Davis was waiting for him. She had been in Málaga that morning and was still dressed for the city in a neat blue dress and shiny patent leather slippers.

"Your door was open," she said hesitantly. "I wanted to talk to you, so I came in and waited."

"That's fine." He took off his wet raincoat and threw it over a chair.

"You don't mind?"

"Of course not, Jenny."

"I've been at the American office in Málaga. You know, where Mr. Kelly works."

Malcolm sat on the edge of the bed and studied her small grave face. She was quite pale, and there were shadows under her eyes.

"Did you have lunch?"

"Yes," she said quickly. "Mr. Kelly took me to a restaurant. We had an omelet and some fish and *flan* pudding. I had a cup of tea, too. It was very good."

"And how did everything else go?"

She tried to smile. "Well, I talked to my father on the phone in Mr. Kelly's office. It was a very good connection. It was just like he was next door."

"When are you going home?"

Jenny looked away from him and swallowed with obvious effort. "I'm not going home. He explained it to me, and it's all for the best. His new wife is very nervous, and the change was hard on her and her children. I mean just getting married to my father in the first place. It was a difficult—" she hesitated and sighed helplessly. "Adjustment, I think he said. Is that right?"

"I imagine so."

"Anyway, she needs time to get used to the idea of me coming to live with them."

"What are you going to do?"

"He's made all the arrangements by phone to send me to a school in Switzerland. It's called the Saints of the Cross. It's in Lausanne."

"Lausanne," Malcolm said quietly, and looked out the window at the sea.

"Yes, the principal is a woman named Madame LeRoi. She's waiting for me. Tomorrow I get the airplane tickets from Mr. Kelly, and some money. He's going to take me to the plane. I have to change in Madrid, but somebody from the embassy is going to meet me and put me on a plane for Switzerland."

Malcolm thought of Señor Quesada and a telephone number he would never use, now.

"Tony?"

"Yes?"

"Tony, would you—" She paused and drew a deep breath, and her eyes were suddenly wistful.

"Tony, I don't know anybody in Lausanne."

He smiled at her. "You'll make friends in a hurry."

"But everybody talks French there."

"You'll pick that up in a week. Look at your Spanish. You sound like you were born here."

"Tony, would you take me to Lausanne?" she said, in a small breathless voice. "Please! If you were there for just a little while it would be all right."

She watched him with a hopeful little smile. but her lips were trembling, and he knew that what he must say would make her cry; and so he drew her close to him and

148

put an arm about her thin shoulders. "I can't do that now," he said.

"But why? Is it because of money?"

"That's an item."

"But I'm getting lots from Mr. Kelly tomorrow," she said. "I could give you some. Or lend it to you, and you could pay me back whenever you wanted."

Malcolm tried to think of something to say that might comfort her. But he could promise nothing, pretend nothing; for he had no more future than a man strapped in an electric chair. He was under sentence of death, and the date of his execution would be set by Jorge or Clarke or Zarren. Only thirty-six hours had passed since Domingo's death, and they were waiting to pay him off for that, somewhere, sometime. And he would be ready, whenever they were.

"Suppose I came to see you in a couple of weeks?"

"You won't, I know," she said, and twisted herself from his arms. "You'll send me a postcard or something saying you had to go somewhere else. And that you might come in a month or so, and then it won't matter any more."

She sat down in the chair and put her cheek against his wet raincoat. "Nobody cares anyway," she said, and then she began to cry, and there was a whole world's anguish in the soft, terrible sobs that racked her small body.

Malcolm stood and went to the window. God, he thought, in real desperation, there must be a reason for the pain in the world.

"Please stop," he said.

"Why? What difference does it make to anybody?"

Malcolm turned and looked at her thoughtfully. He didn't quite dare trust himself now; each of his convictions must be drawn from the same poisoned well, so how could they be anything but deadly? But in spite of this he felt hope stirring in him. He knew there was no freedom in Señor Quesada's smiling insanity. There was no freedom in releasing monsters in life; caging them was the trick. Of course, he could work for Señor Quesada. But he didn't intend to embrace that kind of slavery; whatever time was left to him must be used to make amends. Not to Tani, for she was dead; and you could only make amends to the living.

Everyone had a choice of assassins in life, everyone was given the opportunity to choose the nature of his own destruction; but there must also be a choice of redemptions, he knew now, for no man had ever lived without the chance to dry someone's tears or ease a portion of the pain in the world. And who could judge the ultimate value of these acts of mercy?

And if they didn't kill him tonight, Malcolm thought, he too might have a choice of redemptions.

He knelt quickly beside Jenny and put a hand on her shoulder.

"Listen to me. I can manage it. I'm sure of it. I'll take you to Lausanne tomorrow."

"Will you really come with me?" She didn't lift her head from the arm of the chair. "Will you please?"

"Yes. Nothing will stop me. You can count on it. Have you got a clean dress for the morning?"

She sat up and brushed the tears from her cheeks with the back of her hand. "Yes, yes, I have."

"Fine. Now I've got to go out for a while. When I come back, we'll get packed. I'll bring some sandwiches, and we'll have supper here."

She was smiling. "All right, I'll wait for you. Where are you going?"

"Just up to the Arroyo de Miel. Give me a kiss now."

She put her thin arms around his neck and hugged him tightly. "You really meant it about taking me to Switzerland tomorrow?"

"Yes, of course."

"And you can stay there for a while?"

"Sure, I'll get a job in a chocolate factory."

She laughed. "If you're bringing back some sandwiches, would you get me a bottle of orange soda? Please?"

"Absolutely."

20

IT had started to rain again, a cold heavy drizzle that turned the sides of the mountains black, and collected in shining pools beside the twisting road that led up to the Arroyo de Miel. Either way things went tonight, Malcolm knew this was the last time he would climb this hill; he would come down it a free man, with a never-ending search before him, or he wouldn't come down it at all.

The lights from the windows of Domingo's place were bright yellow rectangles before him in the darkness. He stopped once and looked back at the village of Cartama, and then continued down the narrow street.

Piano music fluttered brightly through the smoky air, and a row of fishermen stood drinking at the bar. Zarren and Clarke and Jorge sat at the poker table, and their small stacks of chips glittered dully in the smoke-streaked light. Pepe was pouring drinks, and the clink of bottles and glasses mingled cheerfully with the tinny music and the soft talk and laughter of the fishermen.

Malcolm closed the door behind him and stood with his back to it. For a moment or so, no one noticed him; then Pepe became aware of the fresh air that had swirled into the room, and he glanced toward the door with a welcoming smile. But the smile died on his lips when he recognized Malcolm, and after staring at him for a few seconds, he turned and busied himself polishing glasses.

The fishermen looked around at Malcolm and moved closer together, as if for safety or reassurance, and then turned back silently to their drinks.

Zarren glanced up from his cards and stared at Malcolm with no expression at all in his face or eyes. Then he put the cards down deliberately, and nodded to Clarke. The Englishman turned his gray face to the door, following Zarren's gaze, and when he saw Malcolm there, his eyes narrowed, and the smile that was like quicksilver flickered along his gray lips. Jorge sat beside Domingo's large, empty chair; he, too, put his cards down and sat watching Malcolm.

Malcolm walked to the bar, and the fishermen moved quickly aside to make room for him. Pepe polished a wine glass as if it were a precious stone, praying and hoping, it seemed evident, that no one would be thoughtless enough to interrupt this act of homely, inconspicuous virtue.

Malcolm rapped on the bar, and said, "Pepe!"

At the sound of his voice the piano player looked around sharply, his hands stopping in mid-air above the keys; and the echoes of his last notes faded and trembled away in the straining silence.

Pepe stood nervously before Malcolm.

"Yes?"

"I'd like a cold bottle of orange soda, please," Malcolm said.

"Yes, right away."

"You needn't bother to open it. I'll take it with me."

"Yes, of course, Señor."

Malcolm picked up the cold wet bottle and walked back to the poker table, and the piano player stood cautiously and joined the silent fishermen.

Malcolm stopped and smiled at Domingo's empty chair. He patted the back of it fondly, and with a certain air of proprietorship, and then carefully flicked a speck of dust from one of its broad arms. Finally he sat down and smiled around the table at Zarren and Jorge and Clarke.

"Three-handed poker isn't very interesting," Malcolm said, as he set the bottle of orange soda down on the wooden rim of the table. From his shirt pocket he took a small bullet with a hole pierced through it, and dropped it gently onto the green felt cover, where it glinted sullenly under the bright lights.

"That's worth as much to me as the chips I see in front of you," he said. "Let's play for it."

Zarren regarded him impassively, but when he leaned forward the light flashed on the cold dull anger in his eyes. "The game is over," he said. "Our game and your game. I promised you what would happen."

"Deal the cards," Malcolm said gently, and rapped the table with his knuckles.

Jorge started nervously.

"It's judgment day for you," Clarke said, and the curve of his smile was so soft and sensuous that it looked as if he were musing sweetly on exquisite pleasures which would soon thrill every nerve and fiber of his body. "It's our turn now. You ruined us. And it's going to be our pleasure to pay you back."

Malcolm smiled at the chips on the table. "You'll be really poor before I leave," he said. He glanced at Zarren. "You didn't understand that joke about the synagogue called Shirley Temple, I'm afraid."

Zarren shook his head slowly.

"You mustn't let things like that slip by you," Malcolm said, and rapped sharply on the table. "Deal!"

They couldn't kill him, he realized with wonder; for it was suddenly apparent to him that these men craved fear as other men craved drugs or women or power. It had been Domingo's secret hold on them. And now they were longing for him to fill the vacuum created by that death.

152

Malcolm smiled and settled himself with a certain finality in Domingo's chair, and there was more than mere confidence and authority in his manner; there was the strong and dangerous implication that the chair belonged solely and rightfully to him; and when Zarren sensed the subtle significance of this, an uneasy frown began to grow between his eyes.

For he knew more than Malcolm at that instant; he knew this was no performance, no play-acting, but a challenge backed powerfully by the potential of this man who sat so naturally in Domingo's chair.

And suddenly Malcolm realized that, too.

"Deal!" he said quietly.

Jorge looked imploringly at Clarke, and then, almost against his will, one of his hands moved compulsively toward the cards in the middle of the table.

"You killed Domingo," Clarke said in a savage whisper, but now his expression was slowly changing, too; there was bitterness and despair at first, but as he continued to stare helplessly at Malcolm, there was something very close to horror in his eyes.

"I didn't only kill Domingo," Malcolm said. "I killed you all."

And this, he thought wearily, might be the only amends he could ever make to Tani. For they feared him now, and when he left they would be condemned to seek blindly for someone to take his place....

"Deal!" he said, and slapped the palm of his hand so sharply against the table that puffs of dust leaped from the green felt cover.

Clarke put his hands over his face and Zarren sighed despairingly, as the cards flickered out from Jorge's trembling fingers.

Malcolm's first three cards were aces, and he began to laugh because he knew he would be home before Jenny's bottle of orange soda lost its chill.

And hearing him laugh, and seeing the pleasure in his face, some of the fishermen laughed too, and Pepe began to pour drinks again. The piano player hurried back to his chair, and when the bright, inconsequential music started up once more, the notes seemed to fly like gay and cheerful little birds through the layers of blue smoke in Domingo's bar.

Malcolm pulled in the chips. He picked up the bullet and

studied it with a faint smile. Then he flipped it from him. The sound it made when striking the floor was small and unimportant, almost lost, in the laughter and music in the room.